SISTERLY ADVICE

"How do you manage to stay in love?" Teri asked. "I was really worried about you and Kenny."

"Things were tough for a while," Maxine agreed. "But we made a commitment and we love each other, so we worked through it."

"How did you know way back in high school that Kenny was the right man for you? I'm supposed to be the smart one—I don't know why I can't find the right man."

"That's because you think with your head, and not with your heart. I think Damon *is* the right one, but you have to be willing to forgive and then forget."

Teri shook her head. "I can forgive, but it's the forgetting that's tough. How do I know he won't cheat on me again?"

"Damon loves you, Teri, and you love him. Give the man a chance to earn your trust, that basic ingredient that all relationships are built on."

"I want to trust him—but I'm scared," Teri whispered.

Based on the television series *Soul Food*
  Developed for television by Felicia D. Henderson
Based upon characters created for the motion picture *Soul Food*
  Written by George Tillman, Jr.

soul food
the series

NO MOUNTAIN HIGH ENOUGH

Sheila Copeland

writing as
Leslie E. Banks

POCKET STAR BOOKS
New York   London   Toronto   Sydney   Singapore

This book is a work of fiction. Names, characters, places and incidents are products of the author's imagination or are used fictitiously. Any resemblance to actual events or locales or persons, living or dead, is entirely coincidental.

An *Original* Publication of POCKET BOOKS

A Pocket Star Book published by
POCKET BOOKS, a division of Simon & Schuster, Inc.
1230 Avenue of the Americas, New York, NY 10020

Copyright © 2003 by Paramount Pictures Corporation

ISBN: 0-7434-6291-2

First Pocket Books printing October 2003

10 9 8 7 6 5 4 3 2 1

POCKET STAR BOOKS and colophon are registered trademarks of Simon & Schuster, Inc.

Front cover illustration by Sergio Baradat

Manufactured in the United States of America

For information regarding special discounts for bulk purchases, please contact Simon & Schuster Special Sales at 1-800-456-6798 or business@simonandschuster.com

NO MOUNTAIN HIGH ENOUGH

one

Teri Joseph unlocked the door to what was left of J&H Groceries, the Joseph family business. Sheets of plywood now covered the places where polished glass windows used to reflect the Chicago sunlight. Burnt debris and damaged canned goods littered the floor. The stench of smoke, soggy newspapers, and mold filled her nostrils as a frown clouded her face.

Bird Van Adams found a pink tissue in her bag and attempted to wipe away the soot on the door handle. The Kleenex was a wad of black fuzz in a matter of seconds and she dropped it on the floor with a look of disgust. She looked up at her older sister, hoping she would want to flee the charred premises as much as she did. "Are you sure you want to do this, Teri?"

"Yes." Teri pushed the door open all the way, and all three sisters entered the store and silently stared at the massive task awaiting them.

The restoration of the family's grocery store had

been Teri's idea. Despite her countless victories in labor law, she had decided to temporarily put her legal aspirations on the shelf in order to reopen J&H Groceries.

"We have to do it." Teri was practically whispering as she mentally tried to locate a starting point amidst the debris.

"That's right," Maxine Chadway agreed, mustering up enough courage for the three of them. "Mama would want us to."

Bird simply reached in her bag for her cell phone. "I'm calling for reinforcements. I don't know about y'all, but I'm calling Lem. You should call Kenny and Damon to come over here and help us with this mess."

Before Teri could say another word, Bird was on the phone with Lem. "Baby, I'm over here with Teri at the store, and we really need you to come over here and help out." She took out another tissue and dusted a spot on the wall to lean against as she continued her conversation.

"We don't need them, Bird. We're going to do this by ourselves," Teri whispered sharply. Maxine just smiled and took out her cell phone, while Bird held up a hand to Teri, signaling the end of that discussion.

"Kenny's already on his way. He left the garage early so he could come and help." Maxine smiled as she closed her cell phone.

Bird looked directly at Teri. "Well . . . shall I call your man, or do you want to do it yourself?"

"Damon is not my man, we're just friends. But I agree, we could use some help." She took Maxine's phone and started punching in numbers.

"Whatever, just call him," Bird said. "I don't know why you didn't want the guys to meet us here in the first place."

"I thought it would be nice for the three of us to do this by ourselves. A chance for us to rebuild part of our family heritage together."

"Teri, save the pomp and circumstance." Bird shook her head as she looked around the store. "Girl, sometimes I wonder what planet you're living on."

Maxine tried to suppress a smile. "Why all the attitude?"

"She was born with an attitude." Although Teri was on the phone, she still heard every word.

"I don't have an attitude. I'm just hungry and I don't feel like cleaning up this nasty store, and Teri knows she needs to stop playing games with Damon and admit how she feels."

"Damon's coming over to help." Teri handed Maxine her phone. "And how I feel about my friend is my business."

"Have you two had any discussions about your relationship?" Maxine looked at Teri.

"We're here to discuss our plans for the store, not my relationship with Damon."

"We need to discuss you *and* the store." Bird looked at Teri like she meant business.

"What we *need* to do is to start cleaning up this place," Teri replied.

The sisters worked steadily for a half hour, making good headway against the mess before the door opened.

"Hey, everybody." Lem walked in the door with a big bag of Chinese food and flashed a brilliant smile at the Joseph sisters. "I bought your favorites, Bird."

"Thanks, baby." She kissed him as he handed her the bag of food.

Maxine peeped inside the cartons Bird was opening. "Lem, please make sure Bird gets fed. You know how she is when she's hungry."

"Please . . . before I have to carry her outside with the rest of the debris." Teri tossed more dented cans into a box.

"When are the contractors going to deliver the Dumpster, Teri?" Maxine grabbed a crispy egg roll and dunked it in sweet and sour sauce.

"Tomorrow. I confirmed everything this afternoon."

J&H Groceries had meant a lot to her father and to the entire Joseph family. Getting Uncle Hardy out of the business had been a major coup for the sisters, but then they'd lost it all during the riots. But the Josephs had survived numerous obstacles and the store was just one more they would overcome as a family.

"You'd better get some of this food, Teri." Bird pulled out more paper plates while Teri inspected the contents of the containers. Pan-fried dumplings, garlic chicken, and shrimp fried rice begged for her consumption. She took a plate and began dishing out some food.

"I understand you ladies are in need of a little help." Damon walked in, finer than the smoothest wine, and Teri's heart fluttered. He fixed his smiling gaze on her and she thought she would melt.

"Would you like something to eat, Damon?" Teri bit into a dumpling so she would have something to do with her mouth and not think about kissing him.

"I'm straight. I'll start carrying some of this trash out." She felt herself grow hot as he picked up her box of dented cans. His muscles rippled every time he moved. Teri went into a coughing spell, and reached into her briefcase for her bottled water. Something was stressing her out again lately, and at times she felt anxious. She hadn't said anything because she didn't want her sisters to worry. She really didn't like to take the medication Dr. Pruit had prescribed, so she drank the entire bottle of water. It always seemed to calm her.

She swallowed the last of the water and looked up at Damon, who was standing in front of her.

"On second thought, save me some." He gently brushed a wisp of hair away from her eye.

"Some what?" Teri spoke out before his words had a chance to sink in.

"Chinese food. It smells good." A warm smile lit up his handsome face. "What did you think I was talking about?"

"Nothing." She hoped she wasn't blushing. For some reason, she felt foolish. Damon was the only man who had ever made her lose her cool. She wondered if her sisters had seen his gentle gesture which had her melting. She tried not to smile too widely, but it was hard not to smile at a man as fine as Damon Carter.

And Bird was right: as hard as she tried to fight it, she did want more than friendship from Damon. There had never been a problem connecting in the bedroom. *It was the greatest sex I ever had.* She smiled at the thought, but no moves had been made by anyone since their breakup and they really were just friends, now.

Teri fixed a plate for him and stood by his side as he quickly filled another box with trash.

"Here, Damon." She handed him the plate of Chinese food.

"Sit with me." He grabbed a newspaper, spread it over the sooty linoleum, and tugged her hand softly, pulling her down beside him. "You look like you could use a break."

Teri settled down next to him, appreciating his thoughtfulness.

"Hello, beautiful wife. And family." Everyone looked up as Kenny walked in with Ahmad and the girls.

Teri smiled as she watched Maxine and Kenny brush lips before Maxine kissed her children.

"Hi, Aunt Teri; hello, Damon." Ahmad was standing in front of them, grinning.

"Hey, little man. How was school?" Damon asked.

"Great." He looked at the two of them with sparkling eyes. "Well, I'm gonna go see if my mom needs some help. See you guys later."

Teri thought she saw him wink at Damon as he walked to the other side of the store.

"So how was your day, Ms. Joseph?" Damon gazed into her eyes, awaiting her response.

"I'm finalizing my plans for the store. You're sitting in the middle of phase one." She was still fighting to hold back the smile trying to take over her face now that they were alone again.

"Things look good." He surveyed the room. Someone had already removed the racks and other hardware, and the family was doing a good job of removing the remaining debris. "When does phase two get started?"

"As soon as we get all of this junk out of here.

The construction company is bringing over a Dumpster tomorrow. But enough about the store, how was your day? Any major deals go down for Chicago's latest and greatest sports agent?"

"As a matter of fact, yes. And when I land this baby, I'm going to need that wonderful legal mind of yours." He searched her face for a response, but she looked away, pretending to be deep in thought.

She was too afraid. They were already close again. She couldn't take the heartache and pain if something went wrong again, yet she was filled with a dull ache because she couldn't fully be with him. Teri sucked in her breath and slowly exhaled, relieved that her breathing was normal.

"We can discuss it later, Damon. By the look on your face, I can tell it's something really great."

"It sure is. It's a big endorsement deal with the WNBA. I know you're going to get bored with the store eventually; it's not enough of a challenge for that mind of yours."

"I don't know, Damon. The store is really going to be more work than I anticipated."

"You can handle it."

Yes, but what I can't handle is you . . . She smiled at his compliment and wondered if she looked as silly as she felt.

"You know you're going to get bored in no time, and when you do, I'll be waiting."

"I haven't had time to get bored."

"Okay, I'll make you a deal. When you do get a little bored—"

"Damon, I love what I'm doing. This project is very special to me."

"Like I was saying . . ."

Teri finally laughed. "I don't believe you."

"I know you." He smiled.

"You're wrong, Damon."

"We'll see. But when your schedule permits, I'll be more than happy to help you out here for a couple of hours and then you can help me out a few hours every week."

"Sounds like a plan to me, Damon. We can use all the help we can get in here."

Bird had appeared, unnoticed. She and Lem were standing over them, wearing coats, preparing to leave.

That's just what I don't need . . . more time alone with Damon. Teri cast her a look of death as Bird gave her an impish grin. *How does she manage to be standing there right at that particular moment?*

"We'll see you guys later." Bird kissed them both and headed toward the door.

"You'll see us later? Just where do you think you're going, Mrs. Van Adams? We've only been here a couple of hours, and you guys are leaving?" Teri stood up to face her sister.

"I've got an appointment."

"An appointment? We were supposed to discuss

your and Maxine's ideas for the store tonight. I really need your input so I can move ahead."

"I know, and I'm sorry. Something came up at the last minute. Besides, it's cold in here. We can discuss everything over lunch tomorrow."

"Tomorrow? Bird." Teri ran things according to schedule and she hated for her plans to be interrupted.

"I got you reinforcements; we accomplished a lot tonight."

"Not nearly as much as I'd intended."

"Lunch, tomorrow. I promise. It's a slow day at the shop. I'll give you all the time you need. Now, we've got to go."

"Go where?" Teri demanded.

Bird took Lem by the hand and led him toward the door.

"I didn't know anything about it myself, until now." Lem gave Teri an apologetic glance. "Later, people." He flashed them all a dazzling smile as he caught his wife around the waist.

"Thanks for bringing the food, Lem," Maxine called out as they walked out of the door.

"Bird, come back here!"

Maxine attempted to run interference for her younger sister. "Teri, it *is* getting late. I'm going to have to get the kids home and in bed."

"Bird!" Teri ignored Maxine and called out

again, still hoping she would come back in and offer them some explanation for her sudden departure. But her voice fell on deaf ears; moments later, she heard Bird and Lem drive away. She looked at Damon and shook her head. "What is that girl up to now?"

two

teri was silent during the ride home and Damon was a little uncomfortable with the silence as he drove to Teri's house. She hadn't said a word since they locked up the store, and he couldn't help wondering if he had done something to upset her, too.

"Are you okay?" he finally asked.

"I'm fine." She smiled, glad that she had allowed Maxine to talk her into leaving her car at the house earlier. "I was just relaxing and enjoying being driven home by you."

"Carter Car Service. We aim to please." His beautiful smile lit up his gorgeous face.

"Damon . . ."

"What?" He smiled again and she felt herself growing weak.

She looked out of the window and tried to think of something to say. "Did that Chinese food fill you up? We can always stop and pick something up for you."

"No, thank you. I'm done with food for the night." He reached out and stroked her face with his fingers. "You were pretty heated about Bird leaving. What was that about?"

Teri sat up straight in her seat and looked at him. "I don't know. We were supposed to discuss our plans for the store, and she came in and flipped the script."

Damon just laughed. "You know how she is."

"Yeah . . . I know. But she's being too secretive. She's up to something. I just know it."

Bird stopped in front of Lake Shore Realty and shut off the engine.

"What's up, Bird?" Lem watched her as she fussed in the mirror with a comb and lipstick.

"I told you we had an appointment, remember?" She smacked her full, copper-painted lips together and replaced the cap on her tube of lipstick.

"An appointment for what?" Lem watched her get out of the car and followed suit.

"We're gonna look at some condos." Bird took him by the hand and led him toward the entrance of the real estate office.

"Condos?"

"Yes. Come on, baby, it'll be fun."

It was chilly near the water and the Chicago skyline glittered against Lake Michigan.

Inside, Bird exchanged greetings with a very

attractive black woman with impeccable clothes
and hair. Her gold jewelry and diamond rings
couldn't go unnoticed. Everything about the entire
set-up spelled money. The realtor, Ms. Wynn,
pulled out a thick binder of photos and opened it
in front of the couple.

"These are a few of the condominiums for sale
on Lake Shore Drive that are in your price range."

Lem looked at his wife, just chatting away with
the realtor as if they had money like Will and Jada.
He looked at the photographs and Bird as she
oohed and aahed over each property.

"Look, boo, what do you think of this?" She was
like a kid in a candy store, and he liked seeing her
happy like a little girl.

"It's beautiful, baby." He smiled at his wife and
the realtor, who was smiling enough for all of them.

"One of these units is right around the block."
Ms. Wynn glanced at her diamond watch. "You're
going to love it. There's a grocery store, dry cleaner,
hair salon, and gym in the building. If you have
time, I can take you to see it now."

"We'd love to see it." Bird was lit up like a
Christmas tree as she took Lem's hand. They followed
Ms. Wynn out to the company's SUV and climbed in.

Lem's heart raced as the vehicle pulled into traffic
on Lake Shore. His wife had expensive taste, and he
knew she was getting them into something they
couldn't afford.

A doorman ushered them into the building and Bird immediately liked what she saw. The floor of the elegant foyer was covered with dressed stone. A chandelier hung over a glass table with a huge exotic floral arrangement in its center, and a fountain bubbled and splashed into a small pond with fish, surrounded by greenery. Several chairs and a sofa completed the room.

They took an elevator up to the thirty-fifth floor, where Ms. Wynn led them into a corner unit. She opened the door to a room with hardwood floors, vaulted ceilings, a fireplace, and a view of Lake Michigan and the spectacular Chicago skyline. It was a two-bedroom unit and when Bird saw the master suite and bath, it was all over but the shouting. There was another fireplace in the bedroom, and the bath had pink and sandstone marble with golden fixtures.

"Lem . . ." She could barely get the words out. "Isn't it fabulous?" She wrapped her arms around him and planted a kiss right on his lips. He felt himself dissolving into her eyes, arms, and body.

"It's fabulous, baby. How much is the rent?" He found the words somewhere.

"Rent? We're not renting, boo, we are buying," Bird declared.

"Buying? Where are we . . ."

She cast him a glance and that sentence was forgotten.

"The couple who own this unit had to relocate to San Francisco. They've already purchased another piece of property so they're willing to let this go for a very good price," the realtor told them.

Bird was already sold as she walked through the kitchen with a Sub-Zero refrigerator, marble counters, and skylights. There was a formal dining room and a small service porch off the kitchen for a washer and dryer. There were parquet and marble floors throughout the apartment.

"I love it." Bird was whispering. "I don't need to see anything else. This is exactly what I want. This is the one."

Ms. Wynn smiled knowingly. "Let's go back to the office and begin the paperwork."

"Okay." Bird was about to trot out behind the realtor when Lem caught her hand.

"Baby, we need to go home and talk about this before we start filling out any paperwork. I'm just coming up on a year at the garage. I think we should wait."

"Wait? Wait for what? She's going to sell this condo to us for a great price. Just wait until I get Teri to negotiate the deal and . . ."

"There you go, putting Teri in our business. We're going home to talk this over, and whatever we do, it will be done without Teri." Lem looked like he meant business and Bird was surprised.

"Why are you tripping?" Bird whispered sharply

as they walked down the corridor toward the elevator behind Ms. Wynn.

"You didn't even talk to me about this first. You just thought you'd bring me over here and spring this on me. But I bet your sisters knew all about everything." He was obviously hurt and almost pouting.

"No one knew about anything. This was just between us."

They rode in silence down the elevator and back to the realtor's office, where Bird accepted a brochure and loan package before she walked out to the car.

"We still need to talk about this, Bird," Lem finally said after a long silence.

"Lem, I'm tired of living in my mother's house. I've lived there my entire life and I want something fresh and new. I thought about remodeling: expanding the bath, redoing it in marble and installing a hot tub, but you know what that means."

"Consulting the family."

"And that means a lot of unnecessary drama."

"I hear you."

"Look, I just got my recent financial statement from Cut It Up. The shop's doing great, and my accountant suggested we buy a piece of property for tax purposes."

"But that's *your* money."

"My money? Lem, that's our money."

"I still think we need to wait. Let me get myself a little more established."

She either didn't hear a word he said, or chose to ignore him. For after Jay was bathed and put to bed, Bird slipped under the sheets next to her husband and pulled him into her arms.

"I'm going to have Teri talk to the realtor."

"Teri . . ."

"Teri will take care of everything. You'll see." She covered his mouth with her full, luscious lips and kissed him until he couldn't say another word.

"Would you like a glass of wine?" Teri took out a bottle of chardonnay from the refrigerator as Damon came into the kitchen.

"Sure." He took another goblet from the cabinet, and she handed him the glass she had already poured.

He followed her into the living room, where he had built a fire in the fireplace. When she was at the law firm he rarely saw her, even though they were housemates. Now that she had taken time off to reopen the store, he was hoping they could spend more intimate time together.

"So, this endorsement deal . . ." Damon began.

She was sitting on the couch next to him. Her eyes were closed and she gave him no indication that his words had affected her one way or another. It seemed as if he was always walking on eggshells around her, never knowing what would cause her to go off in a matter of seconds or what would cause a smile to light up her beautiful face.

Damon knew he was an extremely good-looking man and could have countless gorgeous women at his beck and call, but Teri was different. She was beautiful, brilliant, determined, and independent, and she would not give in to him the way other women always had, women who would strip for sex at the drop of a dime and cater to his every whim. Teri was a challenge . . . which made her exciting; she kept him on the edge. And that was just one of the things he loved most about her.

"So, this endorsement deal . . ." She echoed, letting him know she had heard every word he said.

"Pepsi and Nike have signed on to sponsor concerts in every city that has a WNBA team. The ladies are huge fans of hip-hop and gospel, so the WNBA wants us to put together a series of concerts around the country after the games."

"Really, Damon?" He had her full attention. "That sounds like an incredible opportunity for your company. And it sounds like a lot of fun."

"I am really excited about this, because it's music and sports."

Teri stood up to go into the kitchen but fell back down, practically sitting in his lap.

"Whoa, girl. You all right?"

They both sat there momentarily, staring into each other's eyes. For a moment she thought he was going to kiss her.

"I'm just a little tired from the store." She yawned,

proving her point. She was so relaxed she could hear her bed calling her name. "I think I'm going to turn in early."

"Early?" Damon was clearly disappointed. "I thought we could have another glass of wine and talk about my deal a little more."

"I'm sorry, Damon. I couldn't possibly focus on anything tonight. We'll do it tomorrow, I promise. Good night."

Teri escaped up the stairs, leaving Damon alone in the living room and with free reign of the house. She slipped off her clothes and into her baby doll silk pajamas, and slid between the cool, high-thread-count sheets on her queen-size bed. But the moment her head touched the pillow, she was wide awake and her mind was immediately back on Damon. She had wanted to kiss him so badly at the store, and then falling into his lap . . . She groaned and rolled over in frustration. *How in the hell am I supposed to sleep with him in the house?*

Maxine went into Ahmad's room to say good night. "Finished with your homework?"

"Yeah, I was just reading." He closed the book and got under the covers so she could tuck him in.

"Mom . . . we've got to read a novel in my French literature class. Is it okay if Damon helps me? We've got to do that imagery and symbolism stuff in French."

"Did you talk to him about it when we were at the store tonight?"

"No . . . Aunt Teri was smiling all goofy at him so I didn't want to interrupt, and I thought I should ask you first."

"All goofy?" Maxine smiled.

"Yeah." He smiled and they both giggled.

"You are a wise and sensitive young man." Maxine kissed him and he laughed. "I don't see why Damon can't help you. He is staying at your aunt Teri's house. As long as it's fine with him, it's fine with me."

"Cool. Thanks, Mom." He planted a kiss on his mother's cheek and rolled over with a huge grin on his face.

Teri could hear the television. Damon was watching the news and waiting for the sports highlights. *What would I do if he walked up those stairs right now, came in the bedroom, and just started making mad, passionate love to me?* She played the fantasy out numerous times in her head before she finally fell asleep.

Meanwhile, Damon channel surfed after the news ended. *I must be out of my mind. Damn, I want to be with her . . . I need to be with her.* He gritted his teeth and punched a throw pillow.

But he was glad even to be downstairs with her upstairs. Teri was his best friend. He would never have made it through the Christine ordeal without her support. He still had a hard time believing she had asked him to move in. They might be sleeping in separate bedrooms, but at least they were in the same house.

Stubborn, pig-headed girl. She's up there and I'm down here. We should be together . . . in the same room.

He looked up at the ceiling toward her bedroom and smiled as he whispered, "But there's always the possibility that something could happen."

three

Teri was already at Starbucks, drinking coffee and reading a newspaper, when Maxine walked in. There was a box of Krispy Kremes in the middle of the table and a vanilla latte and an expresso with caramel in front of the chairs on either side of her. When Maxine saw the doughnuts, her eyes lit up.

"Ooh, Teri. You shouldn't have, but I'm glad you did. Did you remember the cinnamon?" She smiled as she slid into the chair in front of the latte and took a sip of the piping-hot drink.

"It's right there in the tray." Teri reached out to sift through the various packets of condiments.

"My sister, the super attorney, always looking out for everyone and everything. Thanks, sweetie."

They had decided to meet over coffee after Bird received several last-minute appointments that canceled their lunch meeting. Teri turned the newspaper over and reread the side she had already read. She had gotten up early because she never went to sleep. She had finally grown tired of tossing and turning and snapped on the television set and then picked up a book. She didn't really want to read, she wanted to sleep. *But Damon* . . .

"Teri, Ahmad wants Damon to help him with the novel for his French literature class. I told him it would be all right." Maxine glanced at her sister before she continued. "After all, you are living with the man." A broad smile covered her face.

"That doesn't make any difference," Teri said.

"Just ignore her. She hasn't gotten any, yet." Bird slid into her seat, picked up a doughnut, and took a healthy bite. Her eyes danced with delight when she tasted the sweet gooey glaze.

"How do you always manage to do that?" Maxine laughed.

Teri wondered how Bird was able to predict the status of her sex life with such accuracy.

"I've got skills." She finished the last of the pastry in seconds. "Ooh, that was so good." She took a sip of her coffee. "I need to talk to you, Teri."

"That's why we're here. So we can talk about the store." Teri closed her newspaper and reached for her legal pad and pen.

"I don't want to talk about the store yet. I want to talk about last night."

"What about it?" Teri was trying hard to remain cool. She wasn't ready to be interrogated by Bird . . . not today, and not about last night.

"Oh, please. We all know what's up with you and Damon. Nothing."

Teri blushed and Maxine covered her mouth, but the laughter spilled out anyway. Everyone knew Bird had no qualms when it came to getting into the family's business, and she didn't care what you thought.

"Lem and—"

"Oh, no." Teri interrupted. "We are here to talk about the store, which we would have done last night if you and Lem hadn't run off."

"But Teri—" Bird was obviously excited.

"Whatever it is, it'll have to wait until we're finished," Teri insisted.

"But Teri," Bird pleaded.

"Come on, Bird. Let's get this meeting over so we can get to your news," Maxine suggested.

"Okay. I'm cool with whatever y'all want to do." Bird hid her disappointment and bit into another Krispy Kreme.

Teri cast her a warning glance before she spoke. "I've spoken with the contractors, and it seems like they'll be done with the renovations the week before Thanksgiving. If we all pitch in and stock the shelves ourselves, we should be able to open on the Friday after Thanksgiving."

"Are you gonna computerize the inventory, like Lem suggested?" Bird reached into the doughnut box yet again and Maxine slapped her hand.

"You'd better stop it, or those tight little clothes you like to wear won't be so cute."

"I don't think computerizing the inventory is really necessary." Teri looked at her sisters. "I thought we could make better use of the money in an upgraded alarm system."

"A better alarm system sounds great, Teri, but we should think about computerizing the inventory. Everything is computerized at Kenny's tow garage. I couldn't imagine counting every little bolt and screw. It really helps if the stock gets low, because the computer will flag it and you can reorder," Maxine pointed out.

"Well, we won't have to count it. Whoever we hire to manage the store will take care of that. That's part of the job," Teri insisted.

"But it makes the job run smoother," Bird interjected. "Do you know how many times I've seen the girls run out of the shop to buy relaxer or dye? While they ran to the beauty supply, the client was held up or they ended up having to reschedule, and that takes money out of my pocket. So Lem set up an inventory system for the store. We buy in bulk, and now the girls buy from me. I charge more than the beauty supply, so I make a little extra profit and my shop keeps its clientele, and that means much more money in my pocket."

"All right," Teri slowly agreed. "I'll look into computerizing the inventory. Anything else?"

"How are we going to let the people know J&H is back?" Maxine looked at Teri.

"We can take out a few ads. But not until we're sure that we can make our target date. We don't want people standing around an unfinished store," Teri explained.

"I think that's a good start, but we need something more. Daddy's store was a part of the neighborhood, in good times and bad. So we need to come back in a major way. We have to show them that we didn't let the riots defeat us." Maxine was clearly excited.

Why didn't I think about that? Teri drew circles on the top of her pad. *I'm supposed to be the smart one.*

"I think we need to have a big bash," Bird chimed in.

"You want to have a party at the store?" Teri was doubtful.

"Not a party, but a dinner!" Maxine shouted.

"Girl, they're gonna throw us out of here if you don't keep it down." Bird laughed.

"You said we could open the store the day after Thanksgiving. Why not open the store on Thanksgiving, and feed the less fortunate in the community?" Maxine smiled triumphantly.

"That's a great idea, Maxine." Bird smiled at her sister proudly.

"It is a good idea, but we can't afford to give

away food. We're coming back into business. Remember?" Teri looked at Maxine and then Bird.

"I'm sure the various vendors and suppliers will be glad to donate items for the dinner. They'll want us back in business to have our business," Maxine offered. "Not to mention it's good public relations for them."

"It's going to take a lot of planning," Teri thought out loud.

"If it looks like we can't pull it off in the time allotted, then we won't do it," Bird suggested.

"We? Just how much time are you going to invest, Bird? You have a shop to run and a family. Maxine, you have three kids and Kenny. I don't want all of this to fall on me. Thanksgiving is only three weeks away. And Damon wants me to help him with his business."

"Damon?" Bird was grinning. "And just what business does he want you to help him with?"

"Don't even go there," Teri warned. "He's got some big endorsement with the WNBA. We haven't had a chance to talk about it yet."

"No, *we* haven't." Maxine couldn't conceal her pleasure.

"I don't have any details yet. I don't know why I even mentioned it." Teri looked at her sisters, and they all laughed.

"When are you guys going to stop playing and take your relationship to another level?" Maxine bit into a doughnut.

"I don't know." Teri sighed. "I think he's throwing me little hints, but I'm just not sure."

"So why don't you just come out and ask him?" Bird suggested.

"Because I couldn't take it if he doesn't feel the same way." Teri drew more circles on her pad, and Maxine took the pen from her.

"Teri, that man loves you." Maxine placed her hand on top of Teri's.

"Yeah, Teri. You can see it by the way he looks at you." Bird placed her hand on top of Maxine's.

"I don't know . . ." Teri began.

"You have to take a chance on romance," Bird chanted.

"I'm not ready yet."

"Teri, that man's not going to wait on you forever," Maxine warned.

"That's true," Bird agreed.

"That's a chance I'm going to have to take. Now, let's finish our meeting."

"Teri." Maxine looked serious. "Don't blow this."

"I'm not going to mess up anything. Now, can we *please* get back to the meeting?"

There was a brief silence, and Maxine knew not to press the issue. "We won't leave you hanging. If you and Bird make sure the store gets renovated and stocked, I'll take care of the dinner."

"Okay," Teri agreed reluctantly. "But I want a proposal and a budget. Meeting adjourned."

She stood up.

"Oh, no. You just sit back down," Bird ordered. "I have something to tell you."

"Speak." Maxine grinned.

"What is it?" Teri urged. "Does this have anything to do with why you and Lem ran out of the store last night?"

"Maybe I'll just wait and surprise you guys." Bird looked thoughtful.

"Bird." Teri was clearly annoyed.

"Don't worry. She can't hold water." Maxine folded her arms and just looked at her little sister.

"Okay, I'll tell you. We looked at some property last night—" she began.

"Property? You and Lem want to move out of Mama Joe's house?" Maxine's probing eyes pierced Bird's soul.

"Yes." Bird was immediately defensive.

"Why?" Maxine demanded.

"Because I'm tired of living in the same house I was born in. It's either that or remodel, and I know you guys would have a hissy fit if I tried to change one thing in that house. You all have houses. We want one, too."

"You and Lem are in agreement on this, Bird?" Teri stared at her over her reading glasses.

"Yes." Bird was still on the defense.

"No, they aren't. Teri, talk to her before she does something crazy." Maxine shook her head and collected her notes from the meeting.

"Well, I can understand Bird wanting to live somewhere new. And she's right; you and I do own our own homes. Have you and Lem already picked something out?"

"Yes." She smiled as she pulled the brochure she had obtained the night before out of the envelope and placed it on the table. "On Lake Shore Drive."

"Lake Shore Drive?" Maxine repeated.

"Bird, this is nice." Teri flipped through the pamphlet and passed it to Maxine.

"There's a unit for sale by a couple who had to relocate to San Francisco. They've already bought a new house, so they're letting this one go really cheap." Bird could barely contain her excitement.

"So what are we going to do with the house after you move out?" Maxine looked at her sisters.

"We can't let it stay empty," Teri quickly said.

"We're not selling it." Maxine spoke firmly.

"No one said anything about selling the house, Maxine." Bird was still defensive.

"We are not renting the house to strangers." Maxine was adamant.

"Who said anything about renting the house?" Teri took off her glasses and laid them on her legal pad.

"Not strangers. I just know there's a family out there who would appreciate our home and not destroy it." Bird looked pensive.

"Nobody's going to treat our home like us." Maxine was really bothered.

"But what are we going to do?" Bird hadn't really thought about what would become of the house if they moved out.

Teri looked at her sisters. "We'll come up with some sort of plan for the house that everyone will be comfortable with. I'll give the realtor a call and check into things, if you can bear to leave this with me." She pulled the brochure out of Bird's hands.

"Thanks, Teri. I have to get back to the shop now. I have an appointment."

"You'd better get back to work, so you can pay this mortgage you're itching to have." Teri gave her a serious look.

Cut It Up might be located in the neighborhood, but her downtown corporate sister had trained her well. No one sat around all day in Bird's salon waiting to get their hair done.

"How did she get so spoiled?" Maxine asked for the both of them.

" 'Cause she's the baby." Teri flipped through the

brochure. "I sure hope Lem's ready for this. You know how Bird is when she makes up her mind about something she wants."

"Lem?" Maxine took the brochure from her sister. "I hope *we're* ready for this."

four

Teri turned off the engine at Lake Shore Properties and paused to admire a vibrant blue Lake Michigan. It was a windy but pretty November day and she couldn't determine which was bluer, the lake or the sky. *No wonder Bird wants to live down here. It's absolutely beautiful.* She had an appointment with Ms. Wynn, Bird's realtor, and she was going to do her best to see that her baby sister obtained her dream house, and for a good price.

When Ms. Wynn led Teri inside the unit and she saw the pink marble bathroom with a Jacuzzi tub, she had to smile. *This is so Bird.* Why had she never thought about purchasing waterfront property herself?

Teri knew exactly what she would say when she sat down with Ms. Wynn. It wasn't a difficult negotiation; the offer was below market and a very good deal for the area. *I wonder if I'd like real estate law, or maybe even selling real estate?*

Afterward, Teri stopped by the shop to give Bird a report. She was surprised when, through the window, she saw Damon sitting in Bird's chair. Her body froze and she couldn't make herself go inside. They were laughing and talking like a couple of old friends . . . which they were. She got back inside her car and drove away before anyone had a chance to see her.

"Why did I do that?" she asked herself out loud as she headed home. "Because I'm not sure what my relationship is with him, but they've just continued on as if nothing's happened." She sighed out of frustration. *No one ever asks, they just assume it's okay with me. They don't consider my feelings. Well, Maxine did ask . . . no, she told me that Damon was going to be helping Ahmad with French.*

"Hold up." She was parked in her driveway now, talking to herself again. "Things are going to get way out of control at this rate, and I have got to slow them down."

Bird carefully shaved off the fine layer of hair that covered Damon's scalp. "Now, how long are you going to stay in my sister's house before you give her some?"

"Bird!" He nearly jumped out of the chair, shocked by her frankness.

"I don't know why you and Teri insist on carrying on this 'we're just friends' bull." She removed the last of the shaving cream and covered his head with a warm, damp towel.

"We are just friends, Bird. And if I try anything with your sister before she's ready, she'll throw me out of there so fast—"

"She sure would. Her and her damn pride." She patted aftershave into his skin. The crisp fragrance was refreshing. "But pride can't hold you at night. Do you have a plan?"

"A plan? Bird . . . take it easy." She was patting his face so hard, it felt like she was slapping him. "You're getting a little rough there."

"I'm sorry." She had to laugh; she nearly *had* been slapping him. "So, do you have a plan?"

"I have been thinking about asking her out." He couldn't believe she had him blushing.

"That's all?" She handed him a mirror, then placed her hands on her hips and stared at him.

"Yes, that's all." He gave her a look that said no more questions. "What's my damage?"

"It's on the house. After all, you *are* almost family."

He stuck a twenty in her pocket. "Buy a little something for Jay."

"Thanks," she said as Lem walked in the door.

"Damon, how are you, man?" They grinned and traded fist pounds.

Bird continued to tidy up her station. "Damon needs help with Teri. He needs a plan. Got any ideas?"

"Good-bye, Bird. Later, Lem." Damon tried not to smile as he headed toward the door.

"I'll give it some thought, man," Lem called after him. "But you need to make that move." Lem turned around and feasted on his wife's beauty. "You running all your customers away like that, baby?" He grinned and gave her a kiss.

"No, just Damon. I can't believe him and Teri. I don't know who's worse."

"You are." He smiled into her eyes. "You've forever got your feisty behind in someone's business."

"Well, I'm about to be all up in yours in a minute." She was just about to kiss him when the telephone rang.

"Hey, Teri . . . you saw the place?" Her face lit up with a smile as Teri filled her in. "I told you it was fabulous . . . ten grand? That's all we need to qualify?" Bird couldn't believe what she was hearing.

She hung up the phone and squealed. "Did you hear that, Lem? Teri's got everything ready for us. All we have to do—"

"Teri's got everything ready?" he interrupted. "I told you I didn't want her in this. Is she loaning us the ten grand, too?"

Sometimes he felt like Teri was running the Van Adams family.

"Lem, why are you tripping? I told you I had this."

"That's my point: *you* have this. Not *we.*"

"You know I mean we, when I say I." Now she

was starting to get a little heated. "If you would just trust me . . ."

"I do trust you."

"This is for us, baby."

"Where are we getting the money, from Teri?"

Teri was in the kitchen rambling through the refrigerator when Damon walked in with an assortment of packages. Teri closed the fridge door and looked at him with amused interest.

"I wanted to have dinner waiting for you when you got home, but I see you haven't eaten, so my timing is perfect." He took a bottle of her favorite wine out of a bag and displayed it with his other culinary treasures.

"No. You didn't bring barbecue from the Rib Shack in here." She wasted no time pulling the container out of the bag, then opened it to reveal an order of tender hotlinks swimming in barbecue sauce.

"Mmmm. They make the best barbecue I ever had, next to my Daddy's."

So much for her plan to stay in her room and read tonight; he had even brought peach cobbler. He was going for the jugular, now.

"I see you approve." Damon smiled and served their plates. He lit a candle at the kitchen table and she poured the wine.

"Daddy made the best barbecue you ever tasted.

We used to love for him to make it. The entire neighborhood would be at our house, because the smell of it just drove you crazy."

"That must have been something." Damon laughed as she continued to share the memory with him. He always wanted to know everything about her.

"Sometimes he'd cook an entire pig. Once we even had a side of beef. Mama and her sisters would make all the other stuff. Collard greens, potato salad, macaroni and cheese, peach cobbler and banana pudding . . . even homemade ice cream. We'd play red light green light, freeze tag, and hide-and-seek with the neighborhood kids. All the time we were playing, we were waiting on that barbecue."

Damon noticed how her expression changed. He could tell she was playing with the neighborhood kids and smelling barbecue as she spoke.

"There were never any leftovers. You'd think Mama would have saved enough to feed us for another meal, but she didn't. After everyone finished eating, we'd play records and dance. Everyone loved the Jackson Five. . . . We felt like the richest kids in the world.

"I wish you could have met Daddy." She looked at Damon. "He would have loved you."

"Really? Why?"

Teri chewed thoughtfully. "You're kind, honest, and extremely intelligent. Enterprising . . . everything he would have wanted me to have."

Now why did I say that? She looked at Damon, but the comment didn't seem to have affected him one way or the other.

"This was really wonderful of you, Damon." She smiled as she got up from the table and rinsed her hands at the sink under running water, to wash the sauce from under her French manicured nails. "Thank you. It was very thoughtful."

Damon stood behind her and rubbed her hands in between his, rinsing his hands along with hers, and she quickly pulled away and reached for a paper towel. Being that close to him made her feel nervous, vulnerable.

He shut off the water and served himself more food. "So, how was your day?" He sensed she was about to break and run, and he wasn't ready for the night to end.

"The store is completely cleaned and de-smoked. The painters are coming in next."

"You guys are really making progress. Did you have lunch with your sisters?"

"Bird switched it to coffee at the last minute."

Damon chuckled as he thought about what Bird had said at the shop. He rubbed a small spot behind his ear. She had nicked him with the razor when he jumped.

"We have to be done by Thanksgiving. Maxine came up with a plan for a grand reopening on

Thanksgiving, serving food to the homeless in the community."

"That's a great idea. It'll be like when your dad used to barbecue."

"It could be, couldn't it? I'm really starting to like Maxine's idea. I wasn't too sure, at first."

"Really? Why?"

"Because I didn't come up with it?"

She looked sheepish and Damon laughed. "What?"

He continued laughing while Teri felt silly.

"You just never cease to amaze me, Teri Joseph."

"Why?"

He shook his head and smiled.

Teri was really enjoying herself. "What if it's too cold for a dinner—where are we going to eat?"

"It's never too cold to eat, and you can eat inside the store."

"Inside the *store?*"

"You have to think outside of the box for this one, Teri."

"So are you saying I think inside the box?"

"I think you have a beautiful mind." Damon smiled and she laughed.

"Okay, you win. But really . . . what do you think of Maxine's idea of doing dinner at the store?"

"I think it's a great idea. Do you think she was

thinking of those neighborhood barbecues when she came up with it?"

"I don't know. She could have, but that's so Maxine, always looking out for everyone." She took some peach cobbler out of the microwave. "So, what's up with the ladies of basketball?"

"I don't want to talk about basketball tonight; I just want to sit here with you and eat barbecue. This has been fun."

"It has." Teri couldn't keep herself from smiling even if she'd wanted to.

Damon clicked on the radio, and the Jackson Five's "Dancing Machine" filled their ears.

"I don't believe it!" Teri squealed as she jumped up, and they started dancing right there in the kitchen. When Damon broke into the robot, she thought she would hurt herself laughing.

"What? You trying to say a brother can't throw down like Mike?"

Teri was laughing so hard, she couldn't reply.

The music switched to Luther, and Damon couldn't have asked for better timing. He pulled Teri into his arms so they could slow dance. To his surprise, she didn't resist.

She thought about pulling away but didn't as their bodies touched and flowed with the music. *Barbecue, the Jackson Five, and now slow dancing . . . I would swear I was set up, but those songs are on the radio.*

She could smell his aftershave. It had combined with his natural scent and he smelled delicious.

Damon smiled as he held her a little tighter. He didn't want to take things too fast, so he decided to follow her lead. To his surprise, she pulled him closer.

I would love to put my hands on that sweet little ass of hers . . .

I can't believe he's not holding my ass, Teri thought as they danced.

But he never touched her once. He was too perfect a gentleman. When the music ended, Teri pulled away. *Maybe he's not attracted to me anymore. Maybe he really does just want to be my friend. The man is fine . . . is he getting it somewhere else? How could I have been such a fool?*

"Good night, Damon." She looked into his eyes and managed to speak in a level voice. "Thanks for a lovely evening, but I'm going to bed now. If you leave the dishes in the sink, I'll take care of everything in the morning. Thanks again."

Then she was gone.

"Now, what was that about?" Damon said aloud.

Damon rinsed the dishes and placed them in the dishwasher. He was nowhere near ready for bed. If anything, he needed a cold shower. He found the special cleanser she used on the marble in the kitchen, and began wiping it down.

Did I take things too far? He looked up at the

five

For once, Teri fell asleep right away. If she had known a little wine would knock her out like that, she would have tried it sooner.

Damon finished cleaning the kitchen and went into the living room. The telephone rang as he sat on the couch, and he glanced at the caller ID and saw the Chadway name. He started not to answer, but he didn't want it to wake Teri if she was asleep.

"Damon." He was surprised to hear Ahmad's voice.

"Hey, little man. How are you?"

"Fine. I was calling for you, got a minute?"

"Sure, what's up?"

"French literature. Can you help me out?"

"Certainly. When would you like to get together?"

"Can you pick me up after school tomorrow?"

"Isn't tomorrow the day you hang out with your Aunt Teri?"

"Yeah, but it'll be fine with her. Mom already

talked to her about it. I'll just call her and explain things myself, and promise to come over and play chess or something."

"All right, as long as it's cool with her."

"How are things going with you two?"

"Things? What kind of things are you talking about, Ahmad?"

"Well, I know everyone thinks I'm just a kid, but I understand a lot. The way things are with a man and a woman."

"Oh, yeah?" Damon grinned.

"Yeah."

Ahmad was one of his favorite people, and now the little brother was giving him advice on Teri?

There has to be some sort of conspiracy in the family. It seems like everyone wants to see us back together, except Teri.

"She hasn't been having any more of those panic attacks, has she?" Ahmad asked.

"I haven't seen her have one."

"Good." Ahmad sighed with relief.

"Could she have had one and I not know it?"

"No, you'd know if she was having one."

"Is it that bad?" Damon's face clouded with concern.

"Yeah. I'll never forget the day I was at her house and she had one."

"What happened?"

"She started shaking and gasping for air. I thought she was dying or something. It really scared me."

"I didn't know it was that serious. I remember your Aunt Bird asking me to talk to her, but Teri acted like it was no big deal."

"Well, it is a big deal. I'm just glad you're over there, in case she has one. But she seems a lot better since you moved in."

"She does?" Now Damon was really puzzled. Teri had him so confused, he didn't know if he was coming or going.

"Yeah, man. She needs you. I'll see you tomorrow."

Ahmad wanted to talk longer, but for now he was satisfied to know things were cool with his Aunt Teri.

"How much longer is the store going to take?" Kenny asked Maxine over dinner.

"We have to be done by Thanksgiving; that's the grand reopening."

"On Thanksgiving?"

"On Thanksgiving. We're feeding the homeless and people with families who can't afford to have a nice Thanksgiving dinner," Maxine explained.

"That's different. I like that idea."

"You do?"

"Yeah. Why?" Kenny poured himself a glass of water.

"Well, I thought it was a good idea and Bird thought it was a good idea, but I don't know if Teri liked it."

"Was it her idea?"

"No. It was mine." Maxine poked at the food on her plate.

"Well, that explains why she wouldn't like it."

"Because it was my idea?"

Kenny continued eating.

"Teri's not like that."

"I'm not saying what she's like, but your sister is used to being a shot caller, and having to take advice from you and Bird about business is not going to set well with her."

Later, as they snuggled together for pillow talk, Maxine lay in his arms.

"Baby, did I tell you why I wanted to work at the store?"

Kenny was playing with her dreads. She could have asked him for anything right about then and he wouldn't care, as long as she kept his tank on full—and Maxine's fuel was premium. Joseph women knew how to love their men right. She propped her head up so she could look directly into his eyes.

"Besides wanting to reopen your father's business?"

"Yes."

"What's that?"

"I want to keep an eye on Teri. You weren't there that day at the restaurant, when she had that panic attack. I've never seen my sister like that and I never want to see her that way again."

"It was that bad?"

"Kenny, it was awful. It was a miracle that Dr. Pruit was there. She's been better since the therapy sessions, but I think her best therapy is Damon, although she won't admit it."

"That's right, he is in the house with her. So have they been doing a little therapy between the sheets?"

"No, I don't think so. Bird insists she hasn't, and I'm starting to believe Teri when she says they're really just friends."

"Teri and Damon? That's a joke." Kenny was laughing. "Those two could never be just friends. If you put those two in a room with water on the floor, someone would be electrocuted. I'll give Damon a call as soon as I have a chance and see what's up."

"Would you, Kenny? Please?" Maxine was practically begging. "Not when you have time, but now?"

"All right, baby. I'll see what I can do. Maybe Lem and I can school a brother on how to deal with a Joseph woman."

"A Joseph woman? Is that how you guys refer to us?" She had to laugh.

"Isn't that what you are? You might take a man's name, but y'all are Joseph women through and through."

six

Teri opened her eyes. She softly thanked God for another day and asked for a special blessing over her family. As she showered and dressed, she tried not to think about Damon and their slow dance. When she went into the kitchen, she noticed it was spotless. He had cleaned it thoroughly.

She looked in the refrigerator and spotted the leftover barbecue and smiled. She was wondering if she should make breakfast when Damon walked into the kitchen.

"Good morning." She inhaled the sight of him in a black suit, crisp shirt, and tie. It was obvious that he had some important meetings scheduled for the day.

"Good morning." His smile could be patented and sold. "How did you sleep?"

"Well, and you?" She *had* slept well . . . some of the best sleep she'd had in weeks.

"Just being under your roof . . . listen, Teri." He

paused to focus on her and she had to hold on to the counter. "Would you like to go to Groove Therapy tonight? We had so much fun in the kitchen last night, I thought you might like to get out on a real dance floor."

He was smiling again.

Who wouldn't want to go with you anywhere? "Dancing?" She had regained her composure but still needed to be sure she had heard what she really heard.

"Dancing. You know, that stuff you do to music?" He bounced in place to an imaginary beat.

"Dancing." She smiled. "That sounds like fun. I'll call Bird and Maxine, and . . ."

He took her by the hands and looked her directly in the eyes. "Is there some reason why you don't want to go dancing with just me, Teri Joseph?"

A zillion thoughts and emotions raced through her heart, mind, and body.

"No," she managed to say.

"Good." He was smiling again and she could have jumped his bones right there in the kitchen. "I'll pick you up at eight." He took half a bagel and kissed her on the cheek as he left the kitchen.

Maxine was on the telephone when Teri arrived at the store. She was surprised when Teri walked in with sparkling eyes, and immediately knew something had happened between her sister and Damon.

"What did you do last night?" Maxine asked.

"Nothing much."

"Your face isn't saying 'nothing much.' " Maxine wished Bird were there; she'd know in a heartbeat if the two of them had been getting busy in the bedroom.

"Damon brought home barbecue last night and we ended up slow dancing in the kitchen."

"That was very romantic. And . . ."

"And then I went to bed."

"By yourself?" Maxine's face registered the shock.

"Of course, by myself."

"Teri, what's your problem? You'd better stop playing games and give that man some, before he gets it somewhere else."

"Oh? Maybe he doesn't *want* any. While we were dancing I thought he'd at least put his hands on my butt, yet he didn't even touch me."

"Did you take his hands and put them on your butt?"

"I've never had to help any other man find my ass."

"Well, maybe you need to help him out just a little. Give him a little encouragement." Maxine was trying hard not to laugh. "He was probably waiting to see what you would do."

"You think?" Teri looked at Maxine vulnerably and flopped into a chair.

"Teri, you need to tell him how you feel."

"But I don't know how I feel."

"Do you want to be in a relationship with him again?"

"I don't know," Teri said quietly.

"Is it that you don't know, or are you scared?"

"I don't *know.*" It was obvious that Teri was frustrated.

"You really need to figure out what you want," Maxine said.

"I know. . . . He asked me out to Groove Therapy tonight. Maybe I shouldn't go until I know."

"Not *go?*" Maxine asked.

"Yes."

"If you weren't my sister, I'd swear you were the craziest woman on the planet." Maxine began pacing the floor. "You're not going dancing with that gorgeous man? Have you lost your mind?"

"Sometimes I really think I have." Teri gave Maxine a sheepish smile.

Damon was waiting for Ahmad when he walked out of the building. A smile lit up the boy's face and he sprinted over to the car.

"How are you, Ahmad?"

They grinned at each other as Ahmad buckled his seat belt, then they were off. This was the first one-on-one time they'd had in a long time.

"Want to grab a few burgers and head over to your Aunt Teri's?"

"Is she there?"

"No, she's at the store. We have a date tonight at eight, but if she comes home early I'll just take you home."

"You and Aunt Teri have a date?" Ahmad was grinning from ear to ear.

"Yeah, I made her an offer she couldn't refuse." Damon smiled, pleased at how well things had gone that morning. After her abrupt departure the night before, he hadn't known what to expect.

"Cool. What kind of date?"

"I thought I'd take her to Groove Therapy for dancing." Damon couldn't believe he wanted Ahmad's approval.

"That's real cool, Damon. Aunt Teri, Aunt Bird, and my mom love to dance."

"I know. She tried to make it a family affair."

"You didn't let her, did you?" Ahmad sounded extremely concerned.

"No way. I've waited too long for this, and we can't have the family along." Damon pulled into the burger drive-thru.

"I know." Ahmad looked relieved.

"So I have your approval, man?"

"For sure." They exchanged fist pounds as Damon placed an order for their burgers and fries.

"Cool." Damon looked at Ahmad. "You're the only one I've told about this. So we'll just keep this between us guys until we see how everything works out."

Ahmad nodded in agreement.

They continued on to Teri's house, where they sat in the kitchen to eat the burgers. Memories of last night's slow dance flooded Damon's mind and he found himself anticipating their night together. But this was his time with Ahmad, he reminded himself.

"So, where's this novel?"

Ahmad reluctantly pulled out a copy of *Le Petit Prince* and pushed it across the table to Damon.

"This is the novel you needed help with? This is what you needed me to discuss the imagery and symbolism?" Damon laughed heartily. "Okay, Ahmad, what's the real deal? I know you don't need help with this."

"I had to make up an excuse to see you. You know how Aunt Teri can be."

"Yeah, I know. So, you want to go shoot some hoops instead?"

"Sure, but not for long. I don't want you to be late for your big date with Aunt Teri." Ahmad grinned and Damon cuffed him gently on the side of his head.

"You just make sure you still get your homework done. I'll worry about my date with Teri."

Teri packed up her papers and looked at Maxine. "I'm going home now. Why don't you go home early and surprise your husband? Better yet, go by the garage and pick him up."

"Maybe I will." Maxine smiled at her sister as she thought of how grateful she was to have a husband like Kenny, and not have to deal with dating drama. Granted, marriage had its up and downs, but she couldn't imagine having to go through the stages of wondering how a man felt about her, again. "I've got a few more calls to make first."

"You still haven't given me that Thanksgiving dinner proposal."

"I'm working on it, boss lady." Maxine gave her a sly little grin. "Have fun tonight."

Teri looked at the clock as she walked into the house. It was only four; she had plenty of time to prepare for their date. Feeling a little stressed, she went into the kitchen and poured herself a small glass of wine, then sat down on the couch in front of the television.

I can't do this. I can't go out with Damon tonight. I'm afraid. She covered her face with her hands and sobbed.

The telephone rang. She wasn't going to answer but she saw J&H Groceries in the caller ID, and picked up.

"Teri, our meat distributor wants to donate turkeys, hams, and roasts for Thanksgiving. Isn't that wonderful, girl?"

"Yes, Maxine." She tried to speak as normally as possible.

"What's wrong, Teri? Are you okay?" Maxine knew instantly when something was going on with one of her sisters.

"I'm fine." She tried not to sniff as she reached for a tissue.

"No, you're not. Did Damon cancel your date?"

"No."

"Then what's wrong?"

"I'm afraid, Maxine."

"I'm coming over." Maxine hung up before Teri could object, and phoned Bird. "Meet me at Teri's house as soon as you can," she said.

"Is something wrong?" Bird was immediately concerned.

"Damon asked her out and she's tripping. Just come over as soon as you can."

When Maxine arrived Teri was drinking a glass of wine, looking like she didn't have a care in the world.

"Are you feeling better about things?" Maxine looked her sister up and down before she joined her on the sofa and poured herself a glass of wine.

"Maxine, how is it that I have two ex-husbands and an ex-boyfriend, and you've managed to stay with Kenny all these years and still be in love with him?"

Maxine silently prayed for the right answer. "Well, it certainly hasn't been easy, but it helps when you're in love."

"How do you manage to stay in love? I was really worried about you and Kenny."

"Things were tough for a while," Maxine said slowly. "But we made a commitment and we love each other, so we worked through it."

"How did you know way back in high school that Kenny was the right man? I'm supposed to be the smart one. I don't know why I can't find the right man."

"That's because you think with your head, and not with your heart."

Teri was silent as she thought about her sister's words.

"I think you've found the right one, but you have to be willing to forgive and then forget."

"How do I forgive and forget when someone cheats on me?"

"You make a decision and you do it."

"I can forgive, but it's the forgetting that's tough. How do I know he won't do it again?"

"Damon loves you, Teri, and you love him. Give the man a chance to earn your trust."

"Trust?"

"That basic ingredient that all relationships are built on."

"I want to trust him, but I'm scared." Teri finished the last of her wine.

"Okay, so we've determined that you're scared. This is good. We're making progress." Maxine poured more wine into both their glasses. The doorbell rang, and Bird entered.

"What time is this big date?" Bird asked.

"He's picking her up at eight," Maxine answered for Teri.

"Well, we've got to get busy. Girl, we are going to have you so fine that Damon won't be able to keep his hands off of you tonight."

"I don't know if I'm going."

Maxine and Bird exchanged glances.

"Have you lost your mind? Maxine, bring that bottle of wine. Teri, go take a bath while I get my tools out of the car. You're going out, because if you don't . . . I swear, I'll hurt you."

Bird looked so serious that Maxine burst into laughter, and Teri joined in.

"I hope you guys saved some of that wine for me. 'Cause it looks like we're going to need all the help we can get for this one." Bird grinned.

Maxine found another bottle of wine while Bird turned on the music, both giddy and happy that Teri was going on an official date with Damon.

Teri relaxed in the tub and promised herself to let things unfold naturally.

"Cinderella better get in here before she turns into a shriveled pumpkin," Bird yelled through the bathroom door after what seemed like only a few minutes.

Teri patted herself dry with a large fluffy towel

and rubbed herself down with her favorite kiwi body lotion. "I'm coming."

When she came back into the bedroom, Bird and Maxine had assembled a number of dresses.

"This is the one." Bird held a short, candy-apple red number with a price tag still on it up to Teri while they all stood in front of the mirror.

"Yes." Maxine nodded in agreement. "That's the one."

Teri smiled as she slipped on a red satin thong and matching brassiere.

"How could I think I could ever go on a date with Damon without my sisters here to help me?" She smiled at them and willed herself not to cry again.

"I don't know what you were thinking. You knew you weren't going out with Damon without me doing your hair," Bird huffed.

"That's right," Maxine chimed in.

Bird tested the temperature of her curling iron. "Come on, girl. This should be just the right temperature now." Bird pulled it out of her oven and went to work on her sister's hair. She kept an extra set of tools in the car just for such an emergency.

When she was finished, she stood back to admire her handiwork.

"You look fabulous, Teri." Maxine smiled as Bird packed up her things.

"You are fine," Bird agreed. "I'd be mad as hell when you walk in the club tonight, if you weren't my sister."

"You sure this dress isn't too tight?" Teri turned to get several views of herself in the floor-length mirror.

"It's not too tight." Bird played with a sprig of Teri's hair until it fell in perfectly with the others.

"You think I'm going to listen to somebody who wears her clothes as tight as you do?" Teri smiled at her youngest sister. She admired Bird's petite figure and the way her clothes hugged her generous curves in all the right places. She wished she could wear things the way Bird did, but she was taller and thinner. Not to mention how people would look at her in the workplace.

"You look beautiful, Teri. Have a great time." Maxine blew kisses at her sister, not wanting to touch her impeccable makeup.

"Yeah, and we want details!" Bird called as Teri hustled her sisters out the door.

seven

It was oldies but goodies night at Groove Therapy. When Teri and Damon walked in, the crowd was rocking to "Oh Sheila." They headed straight to the dance floor and etched out a spot for themselves. Teri couldn't stop laughing while Damon sang along, changing the chorus to "Oh Teri."

They danced until they were breathless, then Damon led her to a reserved table for two next to the dance floor. "You're gonna get a workout tonight, Miss Joseph." He smiled and she felt herself melting. "How about some champagne?"

"That sounds wonderful." She was already enjoying herself. She watched him give a waiter an order for Cristal.

"Cristal?" Teri repeated. "That's special."

"You're special."

"What are we celebrating?" her inquisitive mind couldn't help asking.

"Lots of things." He reached across the table and

took her hands in his. "First, I just want to say thank you. Thank you for being my friend and thank you for being there for me when Christina . . ." He couldn't finish; he wondered if he would ever be able to erase the horrible memory of her suicide from his mind.

"It's okay, baby; it's okay." She squeezed strength into his hands. "And you don't have to thank me, Damon." *I'll always be here for you.* The words were in her heart and on the tip of her tongue, but she didn't allow them to escape through her lips.

He smiled and continued. "And thanks for letting me stay at your house."

"You are more than welcome, Damon. Only the next time I find your Jordans where they don't belong, I'm throwing them out."

"You wouldn't. Do you know how much those shoes cost?"

"Don't try me."

The waiter uncorked the champagne and poured it into their glasses. They both smiled as the bubbling golden drink sputtered and danced in the champagne flutes. Teri held her glass out to the one Damon lifted.

"To friendship." He gently tapped his glass against hers.

"To friendship." She took a healthy sip. "Now, what else are we celebrating?"

"Us."

"Us?" Teri repeated.

"To you and me. Us." He smiled and topped off their glasses with more champagne.

Maxine walked into her kitchen and closed the door with her foot. She had gone back to the office after supper to pick up her files on the Thanksgiving dinner. All sorts of companies were donating food and supplies, and she was so pleased with her progress. She had almost everything she needed from the companies that were participating. She wanted to submit a dynamite proposal. Maxine scribbled more notes in a file. She had already begun to organize volunteers to serve the food and help with the set-up and clean up, too.

"I can't wait until Teri sees all of this." She closed the files and climbed the stairs, happy that she was able to contribute to the family's business. Upstairs, Maxine eased into bed beside Kenny. *I wonder how things are going on the date?*

They weren't playing anything but old slow jams when Teri and Damon finished the last of the champagne. They were so mellow and so into each other, they were content to sit there staring into each other's eyes. Suddenly Gladys Knight's "Neither One of Us" filled the room, and couples headed to the dance floor.

Damon stood up and extended a hand. "I love this song."

Teri followed him to the floor and they embraced, moving to the music. She pulled him closer, felt his hands move down to her behind, and she smiled with deep satisfaction.

Bird was still excited when she ran into the house that night. Lem was chilling with Jay on the sofa in front of the television, with a Corona. She tossed her things on the sofa and kissed her husband and baby.

"Guess what?" She danced in front of him with excitement.

"What?" He laughed as he watched her dance.

"Guess who went out on a date tonight?"

"Who?" They both loved to gossip.

"Teri and Damon."

"For real?" A wide grin lit up his handsome face.

"I did her hair and makeup. She was fine. I told her she looked so good that I would get mad if she stepped up in the club and I wasn't her sister."

Lem laughed. "Did you check out Damon?"

"No, we left before he arrived. You *know* they're just friends." She smirked.

"Riiight. Where'd they go?"

"Groove Therapy. And I bet Damon won't have his mind on friendship tonight."

Damon unlocked the front door for Teri and they entered the house laughing. They flowed together like running water. They always did.

"That was so much fun," he said.

"It sure was." Teri smiled, not wanting the night to end.

The melody to "Neither One of Us" was still going through her head, so Teri went over to find the CD. When Damon heard the familiar opening notes, he smiled and pulled her into his arms.

He moved in closer so their bodies could touch. Teri was drunk on love, and the buzz from the champagne made it altogether lovely.

"Did I tell you how beautiful you look tonight, Teri Joseph?"

"I don't recall that you did, Mr. Carter." She smiled into his eyes as he ran a finger across her cheekbone, then leaned in and kissed her.

"You were the most beautiful woman in the club tonight," he whispered.

The pattern of his warm breath inside her ear drove her crazy.

"And that red dress . . ."

She had never smiled so much in one night. She felt so light that if he hadn't been holding her, she would have floated away. He was kissing her again and she couldn't get enough of him. She had denied herself of him far too long.

"My red dress what?" She paused and smiled in anticipation of his response.

"It's got me saying 'my, my my.' "

They both laughed softly as they brushed lips

together again, and passion ignited them from head to toe. They fell onto the couch together, kissing. Teri helped Damon pull his shirt over his head. She needed to feel his smooth skin and inhale his scent. Her lips kissed his rock-hard biceps, then moved slowly down his chest to his taut abdominal muscles.

She was about to go further, when her mind kicked in and she was suddenly filled with fear.

"I can't do this," she heard herself say.

"Teri, please . . ." His words were soft and kind, and she knew she had to get away from him before she did something her heart wasn't ready to face.

"I'm sorry, Damon. I can't." She sat up and straightened her dress.

"Was it something I did or said?" He was trying to understand why she had suddenly pulled away from him.

"No," she whispered before she ran up the stairs to her bedroom.

She was shaking as she pulled off her dress and dove under the heavy down comforter on her bed. *I never fell out of love with him. I was playing games. Oh, my God.*

She rolled over and wiped the tears that had suddenly collected in her eyes. It hurt to love someone that much and not know if they felt the same way. Not know if he would do something to cause her heart to shatter in a thousand pieces again. She covered her head with her pillow and sobbed. She couldn't risk the chance of him hearing her and coming into her room.

Maxine had said Damon loves me. But didn't Russell and Miles love me, too? They said they did. Even took a vow, and signed on the dotted line.

But what I share with Damon, I never shared with any of them.

She cried until there were no more tears, and finally fell asleep.

eight

the next morning while Teri was in the shower, she tried to collect her thoughts in case she ran into Damon. She squeezed kiwi gel onto her bath mit and began scrubbing her body.

"I wonder if he was trying to seduce me?" she asked herself out loud, "or was I trying to seduce him?"

She thought she heard his car drive away while she was dressing, and sighed with relief. There would be no tete-à-tete in the kitchen this morning.

Bird pulled away from Lem and got out of the bed. As usual, they were trying to have a quickie. Actually they'd already had one, but Lem wasn't full yet.

"Come back here, woman." He caught her by the hand as she stood up.

"No, Lem, I don't want us to be late. We're signing the paperwork for our Lake Shore Drive condominium this morning."

* * *

First Tracy Joseph Van Adams and then Lemuel Van Adams signed their names on the lender documents detailing the financing on their new home. Bird placed a cashier's check for ten thousand dollars on the counter. She had taken all her profits from the hair salon to invest in her family's future.

"Congratulations. You're in escrow." Ms. Wynn shook hands with the couple and laughed when Jay extended his hand. "If all goes well, in thirty days you'll be able to move into your new home."

"Well?" Maxine practically jumped on Teri when she came into the store's office. Located in the back, the office was furnished with antique pieces Teri had found at a garage sale and refinished herself.

"Well, what?" Teri was doing a good job of covering her feelings.

"How was your date? Stop holding out on me, Teri." Maxine put her hands on her hips and looked like she meant business.

"We had a very nice time."

"And what else?"

"Maxine, what do you mean, what else? We had a nice time." Teri took some files out of her briefcase so she could pretend to be busy.

"Did you guys get into a fight or something?" Maxine was puzzled.

"Did who get into a fight?" Somehow Bird always managed to walk in on the juiciest part of the conversation. One would swear she had been out-side listening and picked that particular moment to walk in.

"Teri and Damon."

"Yeah, Teri, dish." Bird pulled her chair right up beside her sister. "I want to hear everything, starting with what he said when he saw you in that red dress."

Teri sighed and looked at her sisters. "It was a very nice evening. We had a lot of fun. Damon ordered Cristal and made a toast—"

"To what? The end of separate bedrooms?"

"Bird . . ." Teri had to smile at the thought.

"Well, did you?" A smile spread across Maxine's face as she sat on the edge of the desk.

"Did I what?"

"Don't play dumb, Teri, you stink at it. Now, dish," Bird commanded.

"I didn't do anything."

"What?" Bird jumped up out of her seat. "Just wait till I see Damon."

"Bird, you wouldn't!" Teri was sick at the thought; she knew the two of them were close.

"I'm just teasing. I wouldn't say anything to him."

"You better not."

"Unless you don't tell us what happened." Bird's eyes twinkled with mischief.

"He was the perfect date."

"Did he kiss you?" Maxine was puzzled.

"Oh, there was a lot of kissing."

"Then what happened?" Maxine eyed her sister carefully. She had sensed something the moment she'd walked into the store.

"I got scared," Teri said softly.

"Scared of what?" Bird smoothed her sister's hair.

"Scared of how I felt."

"And how's that?" Maxine was sure she already knew the answer; she just wanted to hear it from Teri.

"I realized that I'm in love with him." She looked into Maxine's eyes, and then Bird's.

"Did you ever stop loving him?" Maxine moved from the desk to a chair, so the sisters were seated in a small circle.

"I thought I had. But I guess you were right. I was playing games."

"So, what are you going to do about it?" Bird inquired.

"You need to tell him how you feel," Maxine offered.

Teri looked at her sisters with wide eyes. "I can't do that."

"Why not? You guys need to have a heart-to-heart and discuss how you feel about each other, and where you want this relationship to go. Otherwise someone is going to end up hurt," Maxine advised.

"Has Damon ever told you he loved you?" Bird inquired.

"Not exactly."

"What has he said, Teri?" Maxine asked quietly.

"He's said how much he appreciates my friendship and me, that we always have a great time together, and that we're very attracted to each other . . ."

"But has he said he loves you?" Bird cut in.

"No." Teri wiped a tear from her eye.

"Then I wouldn't tell him I was in love with him. A man will tell you when he's in love with you."

"Not necessarily. You can't generalize like that, Bird. Men are scared to death of the 'L' word, and Damon could be just as scared as Teri, if not more." Maxine cast Teri a knowing glance.

"Well, I wouldn't tell him anything if I were you, Teri. Just keep on being his friend, and give him some if you want to."

"I'm not going to be intimate with him until I know how he feels about me."

"Well, you better do something, because if he isn't getting it from you, he's going to get it somewhere."

"Bird, shouldn't you be at work now?" Maxine disagreed completely and felt Bird was doing more harm than good.

"My shop is open and running. My first customer is at ten. Lem and I went into escrow this morning for our new condo. And I'm right where I'm supposed to be for now."

"Congratulations, Bird." Teri gave her baby sister a hug. She really was happy that things were going the way her sister wanted.

"Yeah, congratulations, Bird." Maxine gave her a hug, too. "So, did you figure out what you're going to do about the house when you move out?"

"I'm still thinking about it. Do you have any ideas?"

"I don't recall you asking us for our input since you first mentioned it." Maxine met her sister's eye.

"What, so I'm supposed to put my life on hold while we discuss what to do with the house?"

"Yes." Maxine glared. "You made a decision that affects all of us."

"That's true, Bird." Teri was trying to be diplomatic.

"I thought we did discuss it, when I told you I wanted to buy a condo."

"And we did . . . but it was your responsibility to come up with some ideas." Teri smiled. "I never thought you'd settle on something so quickly."

"*You* didn't think she'd settle on something so quickly?" Maxine was clearly upset. "You're the one who ran over there, making sure she got the best deal possible."

"I'm supposed to let someone take advantage of her?"

"No. You should have just minded your business, and let her and Lem get to Lake Shore Drive the best way they could."

"No." Bird pointed a finger at Maxine. "Now *you* need to mind your own business. You're always telling somebody what to do."

"You *need* to be told what to do, you spoiled brat!"

"You're just jealous."

"Jealous?"

"Hey," Teri said softly. "Let's not fight about this." She didn't want to see her sisters angry at each other.

"Well, hear this and hear it good." Bird folded her arms across her chest. "Thirty days from now the Van Adamses are moving, and the house will be empty. You're always looking for something to do, Maxine—now take care of that."

nine

the family Sunday dinner was abnormally quiet. Teri looked at Bird and Maxine, who still weren't speaking, and wished there was something she could say to get them talking again. Damon had gone out of town on business and she was happy to have the weekend free to sort through her emotions. However, she hadn't really had a chance to think about anything since the house became an issue.

Bird had baked a chocolate cake for dinner. It was three layers iced with chocolate frosting. Maxine looked at the cake and laughed. "Isn't that cake a little flat in the middle?" She took a knife and cut a slice and put it on her plate while Bird watched her. Maxine scraped the frosting off with a knife and discovered the cake was indeed slightly uneven. "Told you!" She held up the knife, covered with the extra frosting her sister had used to even out the layer.

"That's not going to work today, Maxine. I don't care if my cake's a little flat. It still tastes good." She cut a nice-size slice and gave it to Lem.

"If you say so." Maxine took a bite and chewed it slowly. "It's a little dry. I think I need some water." Everyone watched her pour a glass of water and drink it as she continued eating the cake.

Kenny just looked at her and cut a slice for himself. How bad could Big Bird's cake be? He knew his wife prided herself on her baking. If you had to choose the Joseph sister who was the best cook, it was Maxine. Bird, on the other hand, couldn't care less. Kenny knew if she could, she'd eat out or hire a cook. He also knew it was a box cake . . . that was a given. He took a bite of the cake and tried not to make a face.

"It's dry, isn't it?" Maxine looked at Kenny's face and laughed. "I told you."

"Don't pay any attention to Maxine." Lem finished his cake and cut another slice. "This cake is good, baby."

"Thank you, boo." She smiled at her husband, then cut another slice and passed it to Teri. "Here, Teri. You like chocolate."

Teri had been trying her best to stay out of her sisters' duel. They were trying their best to put her in the middle. Whenever the sisters had a disagreement, it eventually would involve all three of them because two would always side up against one.

"No thanks, Bird. I really don't want any dessert." Teri pushed the cake plate away to the side.

"Since when?" Bird met her sister's eye and demanded an answer.

"Since now. I said I don't want any cake, thank you."

"Yeah, she doesn't want any of your dry, flat cake." Maxine laughed.

"Maxine, you're being childish. I can't believe you're causing all this drama over a cake." Teri was tired of their silly bickering.

Amen, Kenny silently agreed.

"Yeah, I don't know why you're causing all this drama over my damn cake. Why don't we get to what this is really about?" Bird and Maxine glared at each other from opposite ends of the table.

"All right," Maxine agreed. "I will. I don't think you guys should move out of this house."

"What do you mean, we shouldn't move?" Lem asked.

"Exactly what I said. You two just up and decide you want to move, and now the rest of the family has to suffer for it."

"Suffer? How does me and Bird moving out of the house cause you to suffer, Maxine?" Lem was getting heated.

"No one's going to be living in the house."

"So we're supposed to put our lives on hold?" Lem looked at Maxine.

"Wait a minute, brother-in-law, I don't think Maxine's asking you to put your life on hold. I think she just wants you guys to wait until we come up with some sort of plan for the house." Kenny was in the conversation now.

"So we're just supposed to take our house out of escrow?" Bird was clearly upset.

"Yes," Maxine and Kenny chorused.

"They can't do that," Teri interjected quietly.

She had everyone's full attention. She looked around the table waiting for the next ridiculous thing one of her siblings or in-laws would say. The feuding was upsetting her, so she'd started drinking water. Now she was poised and ready for whatever came next.

Bird finally spoke up. "I know what, Maxine and Kenny. Since y'all are so worried about who's going to live in the house and not wanting anyone else in the house, why don't you sell your house and move in here? You've got three kids now and there's plenty of room."

"That's a good idea." Teri smiled at Bird and looked at Maxine hopefully, who sat there thinking in silence before she finally spoke.

"You know, we could use the room. And I would love to live here." She smiled at Teri and Bird, and the thunderstorm was over. "Okay, we'll do it."

Kenny looked at her like she was crazy. "Oh, no. Hell, no."

"What?" Maxine and everyone else was shocked by his response.

"I said no."

"Why, Kenny?" Maxine sat down next to him.

"Because that's my house—"

"Our house," she corrected gently but firmly.

"Because that's the Chadways' house, and the Chadways are going to live in it."

"Oh, so it's okay for you to decide what *we* do, but nobody can decide what *you* do?" Lem looked at Kenny.

"That's right." Kenny folded his arms over his chest. He felt like it was him against the whole world, but he was fighting to hold on to this symbol of his manhood. "Over my dead body."

Maxine was speechless as the sisters looked to one another for reinforcement.

"Kenny, why don't you give it some thought?" Teri suggested. "It really is a great idea. You could use the space. Maxine and Ahmad love the house—"

"Teri, just stop it," he interrupted. "You're not in court, trying one of your cases. This is my life you're tampering with now."

"But it's okay for you to tamper with ours?" Bird threw her hands up in frustration.

"Yeah, brother-in-law. Looks like you're playing with two sets of rules," Lem said.

"Of course he is," Bird agreed. "He always changes the rules to fit him."

"I've had just about all of this I can take." Kenny stood up from the table. "Y'all can sit here till the sun goes down and comes up tomorrow, but I am not selling my house." He picked up his jacket and looked at Maxine. "If you're coming with me, I'm ready to leave." He put on his jacket and left the house. Ahmad and the girls were playing outside.

Everyone looked at Maxine, who remained seated at the table.

"So, it's come down to this: my marriage or my family's house. This is your fault, Bird. Every last bit of it, and yours, too, Teri."

She looked at her sisters as she left to catch up with Kenny. They were surprised by her sudden outburst.

"How is she gonna blame Kenny's acting crazy on us?" Bird began collecting dirty dishes and Teri got up to help her.

"Because you started everything when you decided you wanted to move, and I helped you."

"You think they'll be okay?"

Teri could tell Bird was feeling somewhat guilty. "They'll be fine. You know how stubborn Kenny is, and Maxine is just as bad."

"That's true." Bird placed a stack of plates in the sink.

"But we should have thought this through a little more." Teri rinsed the glasses Bird had washed in hot water. She always enjoyed washing dishes with her sisters on Sunday; it brought back memories of their childhood. But it didn't feel right today because Maxine was missing.

"You're right." Bird began washing the plates. "I never thought I'd find something I liked so soon and for such a good price. Everyone is always talking about how difficult it is to buy a house and it was easy."

"That's because your big sister negotiated the deal. We're just going to have to give Kenny a chance to get used to the idea."

After Teri had dried all the dishes, Bird put them away while Teri sat at the table, deep in thought. Damon had just left a message on her cell phone. He would be returning from New Jersey tomorrow.

"So, what's up with Damon? Are you going to tell him how you feel?" Bird joined her sister at the table for some girl talk.

"You said I shouldn't tell him."

"Since when did you start listening to me?"

"You have a successful marriage. You and Lem seem to be so in love. You must be doing something right."

"Why, thanks, Teri. Sometimes I think you don't approve of my marriage."

"As long as you're smiling, happy, and being taken care of, I approve." Teri smiled warmly at her youngest sister. "So, when did you tell Lem you loved him?"

"Not until he told me. But that was me, Teri. You have to do what's right for you."

"That's the problem." Teri looked her little sister in the eye. "Sometimes I just don't know what's right for me anymore."

ten

damon took his seat in the business section of the flight to Chicago. It had been a hectic weekend. He had flown to the NBA Entertainment office in New Jersey to finalize plans for the WNBA project. He had been in back-to-back meetings, leaving little time to think about why Teri had pulled away from him so suddenly, just when they were about to make love. He ordered a stiff drink and felt his body relax immediately as the alcohol flowed through his system.

He had replayed the sequence of events from the other night in his mind countless times, and continually failed to come up with an answer that made sense. He smiled as he recalled Teri's soft, sweet kisses. *Things were going great. We really were flowing until she ran upstairs without any explanation.*

He looked out of the window at fluffy white clouds that looked like cotton candy, and sighed. *Teri Joseph . . . what am I going to do with you?*

* * *

Teri entered the store through the back, left her things in the office, and went to check on how things were progressing with the renovations. The workers had removed the boards from the window openings and replaced them with sparkling new glass. The building was flooded with diffused Chicago sunlight. She nodded her approval to the head contractor and returned to the office, where Maxine was making phone calls. Teri eyed her carefully, trying to get an idea of what her mood was like.

"Don't be trying to figure out what kind of mood I'm in, Teri." Maxine hung up the phone and focused on her sister.

"And how are you today, Maxine?" Teri sat down and began to organize her paperwork.

"You should be glad I'm even talking to you."

"Maxine, we have to talk if we're going to get the store finished."

Maxine dropped a small report on Teri's desk.

"What's this?"

"The proposal you wanted for the opening."

"I thought you had forgotten about it. I'll take a look at this now."

"Whatever."

"Maxine, why don't you just stop this now? You're really mad at Bird, not me."

"You're just as bad."

"And how did you arrive at that decision?" Teri removed her glasses and looked at her sister.

"You were the one who had to run out and be the hot-shot lawyer and get them the best deal."

"That's what I am." Teri's response was cool and firm.

"Fine. You want to negotiate a contract? Sell me your share of the house."

Teri stopped what she was doing and looked at Maxine with a strange look on her face. "What did you say?"

"I said I'd like you to sell me your portion of the house."

"Why?"

"You took Bird's side once again when she suggested Kenny and I move into the house. So if you guys want us to move, we want to buy."

"You don't need me to sell you my portion of the house to move in. All you need is my permission, and you have it."

"So, now it's fine for you and Bird to own homes, but Kenny and I aren't supposed to?"

"I didn't say that."

"You just did."

"Now you're putting words in my mouth."

"You have a house. Bird is buying a condo. And you want me to move out of a house that I already own, and live in a house with your permission?"

Maxine had caught her completely off guard

with her request. Teri looked at her sister thought-fully. "I'm not saying that you shouldn't own prop-erty, but I'm not selling my part of the house."

"Why?"

"Because you're being ridiculous."

"Ridiculous? You're being selfish." Maxine was trying had not to get angry. "It's always your way or the highway."

"Whatever, but I'm not selling my share of the house, Maxine. And that's final."

She grabbed a bottle of water and went out into the store.

"You're selling!" Maxine yelled after her. "Every-one in this family thinks they're going to have it their way. Well, I've got news: this ain't Burger King!"

At the airport, Damon got into his car and headed toward the house, his mind filled with thoughts of Teri.

When two people are as attracted to each other as we are, and truly love each other, that's what this thing called life is all about. Teri loves me. I know she does, even though she never says it.

Teri was still at the store, reviewing Maxine's pro-posal for the grand reopening. She wanted to collect food donations from the various businesses J&H did business with, to let them know the grocery store was reopening. Then she wanted to distribute the food to families and other individuals in the neighborhood on Thanksgiving Day. Maxine had already contacted neighborhood restaurants, who were donating all types of food. So far the store's Thanksgiving Day dinner would consist of selections from a local deli, Chinese, Italian, Korean, African, and of course, good old American soul food.

Teri was impressed with the work Maxine had done, until she read that she planned to utilize the store to serve the food.

We can't serve food in the store. There's not enough room. Where are the people going to sit? And how will we protect the stock? This will never work. She looked at her watch, stuck the proposal in her briefcase, locked up the store, and headed home.

Damon's back, she realized when she saw his car in the driveway. It would be the first time she had seen or spoken to him since the night they went dancing. *I don't know if I'm ready for this.*

She took a deep breath before she went inside. He was in the kitchen, cooking.

"Hey . . ." He smiled warmly and she knew she had to get out of the kitchen immediately or she would give in.

"Hey." She opened the refrigerator and took out a pitcher of water. Whatever he was cooking smelled extremely good. She looked at the stove and tried to get a glimpse of what he was making.

"I see you." His smile widened and she tried to appear disinterested. "Hungry?"

"Not really," she lied. "I'm going upstairs to do some reading. Good night." She started out of the kitchen.

"Teri, are you trying to avoid me?"

She stopped and willed herself not to look at him.

"No."

"Yes, you are. I'd just like to know why."

She took a deep breath and counted to ten before she turned to face him.

"I'm not trying to avoid you, Damon."

"I thought we were having a really nice time together the other night."

"We were." Somehow she was managing to find the strength to stand there and just talk to him.

"Then what's the problem?"

"Problem?" She really looked blank.

"Problem."

"Oh, so you thought because you took me out dancing, everything was on again?"

"I thought we were connecting again."

She gave him no indication of whether she was going to agree or disagree.

"So you're saying none of that meant anything to you?" he asked.

It meant too much to me. It's all I've been able to think about and it's driving me C-R-A-Z-Y. "I didn't say that."

"Then what are you saying?" His eyes met hers and she had to look away or else she would blow it. All the legal training in the world wouldn't save her if she looked into his eyes.

"I'm saying that . . ."

Before she could complete her sentence, he walked over to her, put her glass on the counter, and began kissing her.

"You were saying what?" he asked.

He kissed her again and she tried to answer.

"I . . . I." He had her stuttering.

"You what?" He looked into her eyes and she felt herself melting like butter.

"I don't remember what we were talking about." Teri laughed.

They spread a blanket on the floor in front of the fireplace, and had a carpet picnic. He fed her some of his favorite sausage and peppers with potatoes that he had cooked.

"That's delicious." She smiled and accepted another forkful.

"You most certainly are." He gently kissed a small piece of pepper from her mouth.

"Hey, there's something I could use your advice about."

"What's that, pretty lady?"

"There's this thing going on with the house. Long story short, Bird and Lem are moving and Maxine wants to move into the house, but she wants me and Bird to sell her our shares so she can be the sole owner."

"So what do you want my advice about?" She was treading into dangerous territory. Her sisters . . . the family.

"What do you think about that?"

"You guys already own the house. What's the big deal?"

"She wants to own it by herself . . . the Chadway family."

"Why?" Damon couldn't see Maxine's reasoning and wondered what was really going on.

"See, it makes no sense to you, either."

Teri was so happy that Damon was back, right now she couldn't care less about who was living where, as long as she was in his arms.

"So what is it that we're doing here?" She ran a finger down his nose to his lips, and he kissed it.

"Kissing your finger?" He smiled.

"No, silly. What are we doing? Where is this going?" She had finally found the courage to bring it up.

"Do you really want to put a label on it?"

"Yes."

"Why?"

"So I know what I'm doing."

"What are you doing?" His eyes were patient and kind.

"I don't know." She rolled on her back and looked up at the ceiling. The fireplace crackled beside her. "What are *you* doing?" she fired back quickly.

He chose his words carefully. "Enjoying myself with my best friend?"

Disappointed by his reply, she suggested, "Well, maybe we need to chill out until we know exactly what we're doing."

"No type of intimacy until we define our relationship. Is that what you want?"

He had her mind racing, but her response was cool and firm. "Yes, that's what I want."

"If that's what you want, Teri, I can't do this anymore," Damon said.

She turned away from him so he wouldn't see the tears that refused to stay in her eyes.

"I was gonna mess it up anyway," Teri whispered softly when she heard him dash up the stairs to his room.

eleven

Teri sat in the office of J&H Groceries with her coat on and a blanket wrapped around her. The workers had the doors open while they laid the tile and the furnace was also being repaired. Now it was as cold inside as out. Her teeth were chattering as she took a cup of hot water out of the microwave and plopped in a tea bag.

Maxine walked in and placed her things on the desk. She rubbed her hands together as she stood in front of the portable heater Teri had brought to the store.

"Why is it so cold in here, and what is that smell?" Maxine wrinkled her nose.

"Because the tile men have the doors open to let the fumes out. Someone's also working on the furnace. I thought it would be a good idea to do it today since we have to keep the doors open so we don't get high on that adhesive they're using on the floor." Teri blew on a spoonful of hot tea.

"Then why are you sitting in here freezing, like a crazy person?" Maxine placed a mug of water in the microwave and turned it on. "Your lips are turning blue."

"I was trying to work, but you're right. I can't take this cold or the smell." Teri collected her things and headed for the door. "I'm going home. Call me if you need me."

Maxine stood in front of the heater, sipping her piping hot tea. The family's business and home had been occupying a lot of her thoughts. *I really do want to live in the house. I just have to come up with a plan so Kenny feels like he's the man and it's all his idea.*

She ran several solutions through her head. "He's only going to go for it if Bird and Teri sell their portions of the house. If I have a house, my sisters always have a house anyway. That's the way it is with family," she reasoned.

Maxine smiled triumphantly. *Now all I have to do is get Kenny to go along.*

She called Lem and explained how she wanted him to suggest to Kenny that she and Kenny should buy Teri and Bird's portions of the house.

"I don't know if I can do that." He thought about what she had just asked him.

"Look, do you and your wife want to move into the condo?"

"Yes."

"Fine. And I want to move into the house. Bird was right: we can use the room, and I love the house. Bird doesn't care; she's moving out. Teri has her own house. The house is still in the family, and everyone gets what they want."

"When you put it like that, it doesn't sound so sinister. Like we're trying to run a scam or something."

"We're not. We're just getting some stubborn people to do what we want them to do and what's best for everyone involved, and the house is still in the family."

"That's true. But why can't you suggest it to Kenny?"

"Do you really have to ask me that?"

"Do you really think Kenny will listen to me?"

"Yes. I know the two of you talk. He might disagree with you, but at least the idea is out there and it didn't come from me. He'll mull it over and finally suggest it to me."

"You think?"

"I know. How do you think I've managed to stay married all these years? Kenny is a work in progress."

Lem laughed and shook his head. "Okay, I'll do my best."

It was late when Kenny got out of the tow truck. *How am I gonna deal with Maxine and this house? Is it worth ruining my marriage for?*

He walked into the kitchen, where Maxine was

typing on a laptop. It was late, so he knew the girls were sleeping.

"Evening."

"Hi, Kenny." She looked up to make eye contact and continued typing on the computer. "Your dinner's in the oven."

He looked in the stove and his face lit up when he uncovered a pan of lasagna. "You're startin' to look like your sister over there, on that laptop."

"I could never be Teri."

"And I wouldn't want you to be Teri. I married you. I just meant you're starting to look like her on the business tip."

He sat down next to Maxine with his food and hoped she was being nice to him, and that her mood swing wasn't because she was baiting him so she could really fry his behind.

"Sometimes it seems like your family with you and your sisters is more important than our family," he said.

"How could you ever say something like that? I've always been there for you, and I always *am* here for you. You, on the other hand, could be a little more supportive."

"You mean supportive as in letting you move us out of my house into Mama Joe's house?"

"Yes."

"Sorry, Maxine. I guess I'm just going to be nonsupportive on this one."

"I could be suggesting we move to some other house. You're just mad because this involves my family."

"It always does."

"Well, my family is very important to me. We outgrew this house when Brooke was born. The dining room table is your second office. We need to think about buying a new house, Kenny. We need more space."

He put down his fork. "We're still in the middle of transition at the garage—"

"But that's what life is, Kenny: change, transition, and growth. You have to grow with it or else you begin to die."

"But not at warp speed," he insisted.

"Then get in the slow lane with your horse and buggy and get out of the way. Because if you get in my way, you might get run over."

Lem lay there listening to the sound of Bird's breathing. He tried to fall asleep but his mind kept wandering back to the conversation he'd had with Maxine. He looked at his wife and wondered if she would actually let go of her portion of the family home for a condo on Lake Shore Drive.

"Baby, you asleep?"

"No." She snuggled closer. "What's up?"

"Do you really want to buy the condo?"

"Yeah . . . why would you think I wouldn't?" She

propped her head up on her hand and looked at him.

"Because I know you. Sometimes you get it in your head that you want something, then when you get it, you really don't want it."

She sat there thinking about what he'd just said. "You're right."

"So I want to know if you really want the condo."

"I really want it."

"Are you sure?"

"Yes. Why all these questions?"

"Because I know you," he repeated.

"I know you do." She kissed him and lay in his arms. "I don't feel the way Maxine does. She really wants to live here. She loves this house."

Lem stroked her hair while she talked.

"I love it, too, but I don't want to live here anymore. I want Maxine to have the house. If she has it, it'll always be like coming home whenever we come over here. She belongs in that kitchen, cooking for her family."

"You mean the Chadways?"

"Yes."

"Do you want it badly enough to sell Maxine your portion of the house?"

"I've already been thinking about that."

"Really?"

"Yes. Why do you sound so surprised?"

"I just am."

"I know I'm spoiled and I can't have everything."

"I'm going to remind you you said that." He was laughing.

"Okay. But I really think it would be cool for Maxine and Kenny to own the house. Teri's the one . . ."

"Teri's the one, what?"

"She's the one that's gonna trip. You know how she is."

"But she agreed that it would be cool for Maxine to live in the house."

"She agreed it would be cool for Maxine to *live* in the house . . . she didn't say anything about her owning it."

twelve

Teri was still awake when the numbers on the digital clock read 6:00 A.M. She had tossed and turned for hours, unable to sleep because of her aching heart.

She shut off the alarm before it had a chance to sound and tiptoed into her bathroom, where she took a quick shower. Then she tiptoed back into her bedroom and went through her lingerie drawer and closet without making a sound. She picked up her shoes and quietly inched down the stairs, picked up her briefcase, and closed the front door behind her.

"I made it out of the house . . ." She stopped in midsentence when she saw Damon's car was missing from its spot next to hers. "He's already gone."

Teri didn't understand the wave of fear that swept through her body. She opened the car door and tossed her things inside, then sat behind the wheel. "Where is he? I never heard him leave." She covered her face with her hands and massaged her temples, and suddenly realized she was gasping for air.

"Oh, my God." She tossed items out of her bag until she located an empty bottle of water. "Oh, my God." She got out of the car still gasping for air, and made it back to the front door. Her hands were shaking and she dropped the ring of keys several times before she was able to finally get the right one inside the keyhole and unlock the door. She was in tears by the time she made it to the kitchen. She gulped down several glasses of water and found her way back into the living room to the sofa.

She looked at the blanket lying folded at the end of the sofa and cried even harder. "Maxine warned me. I really screwed up."

Her face was wet with tears and her nose was running. She sniffed and went into the downstairs bathroom for a tissue when she realized the attack had passed. "Thank God."

She looked in the mirror and saw that her eyes were red and swollen from crying. "Get it together, Teri." *I can never go to work looking like this . . . Maxine will be all over me demanding an explanation, and I don't want to tell her about the panic attack I almost had. She'll just start worrying over nothing.*

She applied fresh makeup but it barely made a difference. She went into the kitchen for the chilled eye mask she kept in the refrigerator, went back upstairs, and got into bed. *When did he leave?* she wondered as she drifted off to sleep.

Bird was at the salon, in the middle of a perm, when she received a phone call from Ms. Wynn. Normally she never took calls during an application, but she was practically done. She smoothed the edges one last time with gloved fingertips and picked up the phone.

"Tracy, I called to tell you that the condo fell out of escrow because of your husband's credit rating."

"What?" Bird pressed the phone closer to her ear to be sure she really heard what was just said.

"Your husband's credit rating . . ."

"I heard you," Bird cut in. "So what happens next, and what about my ten thousand dollars?"

"Well, technically, the property is back on the market."

"Back on the market?"

"The property is back on the market; meanwhile, I'll look into some additional lenders. If we don't come up with an alternate source or another buyer, you'll forfeit your deposit."

"*What?*"

"Bird, it's starting to burn." Her client pointed to her head, indicating the perm was ready to be removed.

"All right." She pulled her customer out of the chair and pushed her toward the shampoo area. "I'll have to call you back, Ms. Wynn."

"Damn." She slammed down the phone and followed her customer to the wash bowls.

"What's the matter, Bird?" her client inquired.

Bird turned on the water full force, adjusted the temperature, and pushed the woman's head under the spray. She squeezed shampoo onto the woman's hair.

I cannot believe this . . . Lem and his weak-ass credit. Well, I'm not losing my condo, nor am I losing my money.

"Ouch!" The woman frowned as Bird's fingers dug into her scalp. "Are you trying to kill me, girl?"

Bird, in another world, shut off the water, applied a conditioner, and began combing out the tangles.

I need to think.

She pinned the woman's hair up, snapped on a plastic cap, set the timer on the dryer, and sat her client under it. She handed her a selection of the latest popular magazines and went into her office.

I wonder if I can use the shop as collateral . . .

She picked up the phone and dialed her husband's cell phone.

"Lem, what is wrong with your credit?" she blurted as soon as he answered.

"What?" He was totally clueless.

"Your weak-ass credit. The condo fell out of escrow."

"Get out of here." He was stopped at a red light, with a car hooked up to the tow truck.

"Yes." She was already pouting. She could just see herself taking a bubble bath in that Jacuzzi tub.

"So, what happens next?" He could hear her working up an attitude over the phone, and rightly so. This was serious.

"I don't know. Ms. Wynn said she was going to look into some other lenders. We have to come up with another lender or we lose our deposit."

"What?"

"We'll lose all my money if we don't buy the condo. We can't afford to lose ten thousand dollars!"

"Oh, so now it's your money. I told you not to move so fast."

"Well, you should have told me about your weak-ass credit. I'm calling Teri." She slammed the phone down before he had a chance to say another word.

Running to her sister to be rescued, instead of me. When is she going to let me be the man of the Van Adams family, and not Teri?

Lem drove through traffic with gritted teeth, flexing the muscles in his strong jawline. He deposited the car in the garage, glanced in Kenny's office, and saw him sitting at his desk on the phone. They hadn't spoken since Sunday dinner. He tapped on the window and Kenny waved, motioning him to come inside. He was on the call several more minutes before he hung up. Lem sat in front of Kenny's desk, feeling like he had lost his best friend.

"What's wrong, man?" Kenny shuffled some papers around on his desk.

"Who said anything was wrong?" Lem was trying to maintain his composure.

"Your face said something was wrong."

"The condo fell out of escrow." Lem rubbed the back of his head. "Credit problems."

"What?"

"Bird's trying to track down Teri to find out what we can do."

"Sounds like you need to get your credit straight, before you lose ten thousand dollars."

It had been difficult to push thoughts of Kenny and their latest argument out of her mind as Maxine drove in the direction of her morning meeting. But as soon as she saw the call letters for Chicago's hottest hip-hop and R&B radio station, the battle ended. Inside, she looked around at the numerous plaques, gold and platinum albums for various artists, and photographs of celebrities lining the walls, and couldn't believe she, Maxine Chadway, was really there.

"Good morning, Mrs. Chadway." It was the station manager himself who came for her.

"Good morning." She returned his smile and followed him into his office. She had been listening to the station in the car and could still hear the morning team's broadcast throughout the building.

"I can't tell you again how excited we are about J&H's Thanksgiving Day dinner for the homeless, and how excited we are to be a part of it." He sat behind his desk and smiled at her.

"Thank you, Reggie. We're thrilled by your participation in this event. Every day, our list of contributors increases."

"That's fantastic. These type of projects just make my job easier. We're here to serve the community."

"You're serving the community, Reggie. Now we just need to work on some ideas to get everyone out, so we can serve all that food that's been donated."

"I've got that covered. We're going to run some spots promoting the event. And as soon as those two finish up in there . . ." He paused and looked at his watch. "You're going in the studio with J.B. and Justine and record them."

"Me?" Maxine was still processing what she had just heard. "But I think all of my sisters should do the spots."

"We don't have time for that, not if we want to get them on the air in time." Reggie walked her down a corridor to the studio. "But I can get you and your sisters on the radio live the day before. I've got a couple of shows, including the Morning Show, that will be perfect for the Joseph sisters."

Bird returned her curling irons to the oven to reheat them for her client's last three curls. She could calculate the number of curls it would take to complete a section of hair at a glance; she knew her craft well.

She was unusually silent as she combed out her client's freshly curled hair, recurling certain pieces until every strand fell in place the way she wanted. She sighed softly as she sprayed the hair to seal it in place, then handed the woman a mirror.

"Thanks, Bird. It's beautiful, as usual. You're the best."

She managed a smile as she hugged one of her faithful customers.

"Whatever it is, Bird, it's gonna be all right. The Lord will work it out." The woman stuck a five-dollar tip in Bird's apron pocket and she was gone.

Bird went into her office to dial the grocery store again, and hung up in frustration when no one answered the phone. She dialed Teri's cell phone and then Maxine's, and received the same response.

"Where *are* they?"

She checked her appointment book and saw she was free until the middle of the afternoon.

"I'll be back," she called out to the other stylists in the shop.

Bird got in her car and started driving to the grocery store. She got out of the car and pulled on the door, which was locked. She pressed her face to the window, shielding her eyes with her hands so she could see inside.

Gleaming new tile ran throughout the front of the

thirteen

When Teri opened her eyes again, it was noon. She was surprised she had slept so long. Her mind drifted to Damon and her recent panic attack, and she hoped it had all been a dream . . . a very bad dream. She took off the herbal eye mask and went into the bathroom. Her complexion had returned to normal and she washed her face, then reapplied her makeup.

When she went downstairs, the emptiness of the house bothered her. In all her time living there, it had never seemed so empty and she had never felt so alone. She raced back up the stairs to Damon's room to confront her latest fear, and was relieved to find his things still in the room and his clothing in the closet.

"He didn't move out," she whispered as she returned to the living room.

The sound of her cell phone ringing jarred her. She glanced at the caller ID and saw it was Bird.

"Teri, where are you?"

"At home," she answered without thinking.

"At home? What are you doing at home?" Bird demanded. "Are you okay?"

"Yes, Bird, I'm fine," she lied.

"You don't sound okay. I need to talk to you anyway. I'm coming over."

"Bird?" Teri called into the phone. "Shit! Why did I tell her I was at home? I don't need her over here now."

Teri ran to the mirror and rechecked her makeup. She called her favorite Thai restaurant and ordered takeout, and spread her papers around on the sofa as if she had been working. Before she could finish setting the stage, the doorbell rang. She clicked the remote at the television and headed for the door. She took a deep breath before opening it.

"Hi, Bird. Come on in." She smiled as she opened the door for her baby sister, who could read her like a book.

"Hey, Teri. How come you guys aren't at the store?" Bird looked her up and down.

"I decided to work from home this morning." Teri managed a faint smile.

"Are you okay, Teri?" Bird was still looking at her strangely as she carefully moved a few of Teri's papers and sat on the sofa.

"I told you I'm fine."

"Did I wake you up or something?" Bird couldn't

put her finger on it, but she sensed something wasn't right.

"I had dozed off before you called."

"Oh. . . . Where's Damon?"

Oh my God, Bird hasn't been talking to him, has she? No wonder she's full of questions. "He's at work, Bird. Speaking of which, why aren't you at the shop?"

"Because I've been out looking for y'all. Where's Maxine?"

"She probably had a meeting outside of the store. Didn't you mention you wanted to talk to me about something?"

Before she could answer, the doorbell rang. It was the delivery boy with the Thai food. She searched for her purse and remembered she had left it and its contents, along with her medication, in the car. She returned to the living room and was relieved to see her keys on the coffee table. She snatched them up and ran out to the car, gathered the contents of her purse, and paid for the delivery. Bird watched her walk back in with the food.

"You're acting weird, Teri."

"You're the one who's acting weird, Bird. You're over here in the middle of the day. Have you eaten?" Teri carried the bag of food into the kitchen.

"No." She followed Teri into the kitchen and watched her take the cartons of food out of the shopping bag. "I'm not hungry."

Teri wasn't hungry, either, but she had to do something to keep Bird's focus off of her. She served a small portion of everything onto two plates and pushed one toward Bird, then found chopsticks in the bag and handed a pair to Bird.

She picked up some of the pad thai noodles and forced herself to eat them. "Since when aren't you hungry?"

"Since my condo fell out of escrow."

"What?" Teri's chopsticks fell onto her plate.

"Lem's got a lousy credit rating." Bird wasn't as angry as she had been earlier, when she first heard the news. She knew her sister would take care of everything, now that she had found her.

"I thought you guys prepared for this. If you had prepared, you would have known about Lem's credit."

"I thought if I had the money, as well as a successful business, it would be no problem."

"It shouldn't have been—but your husband doesn't have the cleanest background."

"We know that, Teri." Bird picked at a shrimp.

"What did the realtor say?"

"She said the property is back on the market."

"I'm sure she'll find some sort of first-time-buyers' program that will be a little more lenient. I'll do some research and see what's available."

"Thanks, Teri." She broached the other question she'd had for her sister. "Can I use my shop as collateral?"

"You already have. That's how you qualified."

"Well, can't they take Lem off and just use me?"

"Are you sure you want to do that? It might cause problems between you two, because the property would be in your name."

"We both want that condo. I'll talk it over with Lem and hopefully he'll agree."

In his office, Damon opened the newspaper to the real estate section and perused the column for available apartments. He hadn't been able to sleep all night, thinking about Teri, and decided it was really the best thing for both of them, for him to move out.

I've got to move on, and as long as I'm living in that house with her, I won't. She made herself perfectly clear last night. She's not interested in having a relationship with me.

He yawned as he circled several of the listings. He had finally left the house at five in the morning for the gym, where he had put himself through a grueling workout to clear his mind. By the time he arrived at work, he knew what he had to do.

He stared out of his window at the sunless, cold November day. As far as he could see, everything was gray.

He picked up the phone and called the first apartment on the list.

fourteen

teri walked Bird out to her car and handed her the leftovers, practically everything from their Thai food lunch. Neither of them had been particularly hungry.

"You and Lem eat the rest of this for dinner. You really liked those noodles." She smiled as Bird opened the car door with her remote. "And don't worry about the condo. Everything's going to be fine."

"Thanks, Teri." Bird fastened her seat belt and looked at Teri, who motioned for her to let down the window.

"How many more clients do you have this afternoon?"

"Just two. It's a slow day."

"Yeah, it is a little slow." Teri glanced at her watch and was surprised that it was just 1:30.

"Okay, I'm out." Bird leaned out of the window and kissed her sister on the cheek, then started backing out of the driveway. "Go inside before you catch a cold," she called before she drove away.

Teri was chilled by the time she went back in the house, but the cold air had been refreshing. Despite the circumstances, Bird's unexpected visit had turned out to be a welcome intrusion.

She had settled back under the blanket to warm herself when she caught a whiff of Damon's cologne on it. She froze, then tossed it off and ran up the stairs to change, her mind buzzing. Jeans and a heavy turtleneck sweater would keep her warm at the store.

Without thinking, she picked up the phone and speed-dialed Damon at the office to share her latest revelation. His personal line rang several times, then his voice mail kicked in. She listened to his message and smiled before she hung up. Sometimes she would call his voice mail just to hear his voice. She dialed the main number for Moore, Freeman and spoke to the receptionist.

"Is Mr. Carter still at lunch?"

"Yes, Ms. Joseph. He has a meeting at two, so he should be back in the office any minute."

"Thank you. There's no message. I'm going to stop by and speak to him personally."

Maxine arrived at the store and was surprised to find it empty. She was eager to share her news about the radio station and was disappointed that Teri wasn't around. "Where is that girl? She's supposed to be here."

She quickly read a note that a trucking company had stuck on the back door, informing them of an attempted delivery. Then she finally succeeded in reaching Teri on her cell phone.

"Teri, where are you?" She looked around the small office, still trying to determine if her sister had been there.

"I'm on my way. I have a quick appointment and then I'll be right there."

"We missed a delivery. Have you been in today?"

"No, I was working from home. What did I miss?"

"Something from UPS."

"Call them and reschedule it. Is there something you needed?"

"No. I was just wondering where you were. Is everything okay?"

"Why does everyone keep asking me that?" She tried hard not to sound annoyed. "I'm fine, Maxine."

"Okay, Teri, spare me the attitude, because I do have a right to check on my sister."

"Did I have an attitude? I'm sorry, Maxine. It's been a stressful day. How are you?"

"Great! I can't wait to tell you about my meeting at the radio station."

"Radio station? Maxine what are you up to now?"

"It's a wonderful opportunity for the store, and you'll love it. I'll tell you all about it when you get here."

"Tell me now."

"When you get here."

"Just tell me what you were doing at the radio station. Please?"

"Okay." Maxine was extremely excited. "The station's coming out to broadcast live from the store on Thanksgiving. I even recorded some promotional spots with the Morning Team! They're going to start playing them a week before Thanksgiving."

Teri thought about that. "Those radio spots are going to attract people from all over the city."

"Isn't that wonderful?"

"Will we have enough food to feed all of these people?"

"We have plenty of food, Teri."

"Enough to feed the entire city of Chicago?"

"The entire city of Chicago isn't coming." Maxine laughed.

"Okay, well, half the city. We'd better make sure we have enough people to handle the serving. I'm not dishing out food to half of Chicago."

"Teri, don't be ridiculous."

Teri pulled into a visitor's spot in Moore, Freeman's parking garage. "I'm at my appointment now; I have to go. We'll continue this discussion later."

"Where are you?"

"At my appointment."

"Where?"

"Maxine."

"Okay, you aren't going to tell me. Just hurry up and come in, so I can tell you all about the interviews we're going to do."

"Interviews?"

" 'Bye, Teri. Have a nice appointment."

Teri shook her head and turned off her cell phone.

She freshened her lip gloss on the ride up in the elevator. She was cool, very composed, and surprisingly felt no emotion whatsoever when she walked in the doors. This was the first time she had been in the office since she resigned. Damon, however, operated Carter Sports Management out of their offices.

She walked up to the receptionist desk, poised and confident as ever. She already knew she was sorely missed. Damon had overheard a conversation between several of the partners and she had been the topic of discussion. They would never be able to find a labor attorney as experienced or as qualified as Teri Joseph, he'd heard say.

"Has Mr. Carter returned from lunch yet?"

"No, Ms. Joseph. He's running a little late. He asked me to have you wait in his office."

"Thank you." As she made her way to Damon's office, she could feel and see heads turning. She was glad she was wearing jeans. They were tight, faded, extremely comfortable, and Damon loved them on her. No one would think she was job hunting in this attire.

The partners had moved Damon to an office with a view. He had told her about it, but she really hadn't been interested in anything going on at Moore, Freeman. She stepped in the room and was amazed by the view. She couldn't help the twinge of jealousy she felt.

She stepped up to the window and realized the dark gray line across the horizon was Lake Michigan. When she turned around, she smiled at a photo of her and Damon that had been taken at a Fourth of July picnic. She knew every woman in the law firm had seen that photo. She also knew some woman was probably always in and out of his office. She started to sit in one of the chairs in front of the desk, but decided to sit in his chair because it was more comfortable.

Teri listened to phones that constantly rang, watched assistants run back and forth to make copies, and noticed several partners returning from lunch.

I miss this environment . . . the intensity, the aggression, and the competition . . . the knowledge. I miss law. It had taken her a while to come to this conclusion. *I'm not a person who lives in denial . . . what's wrong with me? Why do I keep denying myself of things I really love?*

*Because you're afraid they won't meet your expecta-
tions.* She could hear Dr. Pruit's words echoing in
her mind.

She shook her head as if she were trying to shake
his words out. She took out her planner and made a
note to call some former colleagues, although she
knew she wouldn't forget. It was suddenly obvious
to her that it was time to get back to work as an
attorney. She looked at her watch and saw that it
was ten past two. *Damon, where are you?*

Teri scanned the desk, looking for something to
read. There was a pad with numbers and notes, but
she didn't look at that. She didn't like people reading things on her desk and she returned the cour-
tesy. She spotted a newspaper and pulled it out
from under a stack of *Sports Illustrated* magazines.
Normally, she would have read the paper before
she left for work in the morning, but nothing
about today had been normal.

The want ads. She noticed numerous circled
items and looked closer . . . and gasped. Suddenly,
she felt as if someone had just punched her in the
stomach really hard.

Teri carefully replaced the newspaper and tried
to cover any signs that would inform Damon that
she had been there. Then she slipped out of his
office, down the hall, and into the elevator foyer,
where she impatiently pressed the down button several times.

Should she take the stairs? She had to get out of there as quickly as possible. But just then, the elevator finally arrived . . . actually, two of them at the same time. As she stood waiting for her elevator to empty, she looked up to see Damon and a pretty young woman exiting the other elevator. They were both so busy smiling and laughing that he almost didn't notice her.

If he's not getting it from you, he's getting it from somewhere else. Bird's words of advice suddenly ran through her mind.

"Teri!" He was surprised that she was leaving, especially since she hadn't even spoken. His secretary had phoned to inform him that she was waiting, but his meeting had run over. "Teri, where are you going?"

She made eye contact just as her elevator's doors closed. Damon, frustrated, couldn't understand the reason behind the intense pain he had read from her eyes and face.

Kenny was changing a tire on one of the trucks when Lem returned to the garage.

"I see you got your face correct." Kenny looked up at him.

"I had to clear my head, so I went to grab a bite to eat." A brilliant smile lit up his handsome face. "I got you some rib tips from the Rib Shack. You down?"

"Rib tips from the Shack? You don't have to call me twice." Kenny put down his wrench and wiped the grease off of his hands.

He took the container of food from his brother-in-law and headed for his office. Kenny looked like he was in heaven as he polished off the ribs.

"Good looking out, brother-in-law." Kenny grinned and toasted him with a can of soda.

Lem just smiled and wondered how to say what he needed to say.

"So, did you get some advice on your credit?"

"There's nothing I can really do. What will be will be. But I've been thinking about our conversation at Sunday dinner."

"What was that, man?"

"About Mama Joe's house."

"What about it?" Kenny's tone was slowly changing.

"Have you given it any thought? You and Maxine moving in there?"

"Not really." He got up and started rambling through one of the file cabinets.

"Look, Kenny. I'm not saying this because I want you guys to move in there so that we can move out. To be honest, I care because it's important to Bird and to all the sisters." Even though Kenny was still in the file cabinet, Lem could tell he was listening.

"I never had a real family, not until I became part of this one. And I think things like the house staying in the family are important. Maxine loves that house. It would be like having Mama Joe in the house all over again. It's bigger, and it's closer to your business. And Bird is willing to sell you guys her share. She wants Maxine to have the house, too."

"She does?" Kenny closed the file cabinet and looked at Lem.

"Yeah, man. We talked about it the other night, and she would love to see you guys living in the house."

"And she's willing to sell us her share?" Kenny sat down at his desk. Lem could tell he was really thinking.

"I'm on your side. I don't think you should sell your house and not own another one. Black people don't own enough land or businesses already."

"I hear you, and you're right. About the family thing, too. I was never really part of a family, either, until I married Maxine. Not a real one, with the love and values of the Josephs."

The brothers-in-law sat in silence for several moments.

"Maxine was talking about our family and our business the other night. How I would want to have one of my kids run this business one day, and that's why she had to work on the store—because it belonged to her father."

"Maxine is all about family and the community."

"You guys didn't happen to mention any of this

to Teri, did you?" Kenny secretly prayed Lem would say yes.

"That's one mountain you and Maxine are going to have to move yourselves. We've got your back, but Bird already said Teri could cause problems."

"I hear you loud and clear, brother-in-law. Teri can be real cool, but she can also be extremely difficult." Kenny rubbed his head while he spoke.

"And then she might want to sell her share. You never know with Teri. We'll just have to wait and see." Lem tore a sheet of paper from his pad, crumpled it, and tossed it toward the trash like a basketball.

Now that Lem had succeeded in getting Kenny to listen to him, he could see how much his and Bird's decision to move was affecting everyone. But that was one of the few downsides of being in a family as close as the Josephs. There was really no decision made independently of another family member. It also made Teri's decision about her share in Mama Joe's house extremely critical now.

fifteen

Teri sat in her car in the parking lot, forcing herself to consume water to calm down. Water and deep breathing had always been successful in getting her through a panic attack before she started taking Dr. Pruit's medication. After her morning escapade, she had stuck the pills in her handbag. Now she took out the bottle and looked at it. She didn't want to take the medicine and drive. *And I have to drive. I have got to get out of here.* She gripped the steering wheel tightly and managed to control her breathing.

She started up the car and slowly pulled out of the parking garage. As soon as she hit the street, the heavens opened and poured out a deluge of rain. In a matter of minutes, water was running down the street like a river.

No wonder he didn't have time to see me. He's already got someone else to keep him company. He probably had her all along. And . . . he's moving out.

Realizing she needed to calm down more so she could focus on her driving, Teri pulled over to the side of the street. Checking her cell phone, she saw she had three messages. She ignored them and phoned Maxine at the store.

"Hey, Maxine, this rain is really coming down so I'm not going to drive over to the store today. If there's anything you really need me to take a look at, you can fax it to the house."

"Nothing pressing. I just can't wait to talk to you about the promotions for the dinner."

"We'll discuss it later, Maxine."

"So, I can't change your mind about coming in?" Maxine was hopeful.

"No. The day's almost over, and now it's raining cats and dogs. Why don't you take off early so you can spend some time with Ahmad and the girls . . . and Kenny? Did you get things straight with him?"

"Look who's talking. Did you get things straight with Damon yet?"

"Things are fine with Damon. Look, I have to go."

"Teri, I don't believe you! You forgot about Ahmad's birthday dinner tonight."

Teri clasped a hand to her mouth. "No, I didn't."

"Yes, you did."

"It was on my mind, because I still have to get him a present," she lied.

"My house, tonight at seven. Ahmad wants us to dress up."

"What?"

"Keisha's coming and some friends from school."

"He's really something, isn't he? I'll see you later, Maxine." Teri cut her cell phone off and looked at the rain that continued to pour out of the sky, pelting the car, the ground, and the entire city.

Maxine walked to the front of the store and looked out of the window. She thought about Ahmad walking home from the bus stop, and decided to leave early so she could pick him up and start his birthday dinner. She was just about to walk out the door when the store's telephone rang.

"Maxine, it's Damon. Is Teri there?" He sounded really anxious.

"No, but you can reach her on her cell phone."

"I tried her cell phone and she's not answering."

"She just called me to tell me she wasn't coming to the store. Is something wrong?"

"No. Just tell her to call me if you talk to her again."

"Damon, are you sure there's nothing you want to talk about?"

"No, Maxine. Is there something you want to talk about?"

"I did some really great spots this morning with J.B. and Justine at the radio station, promoting the reopening and our Thanksgiving Day dinner for the homeless."

"You go, girl. You're such a star."

He had her grinning ear to ear. "I'll see you at Ahmad's birthday dinner tonight?"

"Ahmad's birthday? Oh, no. I completely forgot, and I just found out I have to go out of town in the morning."

"Don't tell me, tell Ahmad. He'll be so disappointed."

Now she knew something was going on with him and Teri. There was no way both of them could have forgotten Ahmad's birthday.

"I really want to come, Maxine, but I've got a lot of work to do. If I come by there I'll stay longer than I intended, and you know the rest."

"I'll kick you out at a decent hour. I promise."

"I'm sorry, but I'm going to have to pass." He really wanted to go, but since he and Teri had called off whatever relationship they had, he felt awkward about attending a big family gathering.

"Is that your final answer?"

"Yes. Tell Ahmad to call me when he gets in from school."

Despite the downpour, Teri headed toward the mall. She found a spot close to the main entrance and grabbed her umbrella from the backseat, then made a dash for the door.

Inside, she looked up and down the store-lined corridor and tried to decide where to go first. It was unusually quiet and still; there were only a few seniors and mothers with babies in strollers. Teri was always at work during the day and so she shopped mostly on weekends.

She went into Ahmad's favorite stores and purchased the latest Timberlands, and a sweater. She smiled as the saleslady folded the designer sweater and placed it in a box.

She still had quite a bit of time to kill if she wanted to avoid running into Damon at the house, so she opted for the bookstore. She could spend hours browsing.

Maxine was waiting in the car when Ahmad's bus pulled up.

"Mom." His face lit up with a bright smile when he saw her waving from the car. "Thanks for picking me up. I didn't wear my slicker."

"Happy birthday, sweetie. I know it's raining, but we won't let it spoil your party."

"It'll be great as long as everyone comes."

"Damon said he won't be able to make it, because he's going out of town. He wants you to call him. See if you can change his mind."

When they got home, Maxine stood at the kitchen sink, holding the cordless phone to her ear with her shoulder while she cleaned the collards. She tried to call Teri but failed to reach her. The she phoned Bird, who was just finishing up her last client.

"Have you talked to Teri today?" Maxine placed

the cleaned greens on the stove and began peeling potatoes. Her fingers moved the paring knife swiftly from years of experience.

"Not since lunch."

"You guys had lunch together?" She tried not to sound jealous.

"Yes. I went by her house to discuss something and she had all this Thai food."

"What were you discussing?"

Bird hesitated, trying to decide if she should tell her.

"That's okay, Bird. You and Teri can keep your little secrets." Maxine wondered if Teri had told her anything about Damon.

"We don't have any secrets, Maxine. I just didn't know if you would care."

"Care about what?" She put the potatoes on to boil and took out the chicken.

Bird hesitated again before she blurted out her response. "My condo fell out of escrow."

"What?"

"Because of Lem's credit rating. The property is back on the market, and we have to find another lending source."

"I'm sorry, Bird. How could you think I wouldn't care?"

"Well, you've been acting real funny ever since we said we were going to buy it. We might lose our ten thousand dollars, too."

"Bird, I'm so sorry. I can't believe you wouldn't think I'd care about something like this. What did Teri say?"

"She said everything would work out. That we should qualify for some first-time-buyers' programs."

"Good. Well, don't forget Ahmad's party at seven."

"Now why would I forget Ahmad's party?"

"Teri did."

"Well, Teri's been acting a little strange all day."

Maxine hung up, put on the rest of the food, and came into the living room to talk to her son.

"How'd you make out?"

"Dad called to say he's on his way home, and Damon's coming, too."

"Perfect. You need to start getting dressed."

She went back into the kitchen to check on the dinner. "I don't know what's up with you, Teri Joseph, but forgetting your nephew's birthday isn't like you."

sixteen

teri finished choosing a card for Ahmad and afterward went into Neiman Marcus. It was one of those days when there were several things that caught her eye, and she found a wonderful outfit on sale. She tried on countless pairs of shoes until she found the perfect pair, selected a matching purse, a new shade of lipstick and a new fragrance.

Then she went into the fitting room and made a complete transformation. She had found the perfect little black cocktail dress and the new Prada shoes looked great with it. She played with her hair, wishing it had Bird's expert touch, and managed to pin it up decently.

She stopped for costume jewelry, and a black wool coat that was a wonderful addition to her wardrobe. When she left, carrying her jeans and turtleneck in a department store shopping bag, she was glad to see the rain had finally stopped.

* * *

Maxine swirled the last of the chocolate frosting across the side of the cake as the doorbell rang. She licked a dab of frosting from her finger, and quickly rinsed her hands.

She opened the door to find Damon standing there.

"I hear you're feeding the homeless tonight." He smiled and she knew her sister had to be brain damaged for not letting that man sleep in her bedroom.

"Come in, silly." She laughed.

"For you, madam." He handed her a bouquet of mixed flowers.

"Damon, you didn't have to . . ." She shut the door and he followed her into the kitchen, where she arranged the flowers in a vase.

"Yes, I did have to. It's not every day I get invited to dinner by Superwoman. Where's the birthday boy?"

"In the family room with his friends, having drinks and appetizers. How did he talk you into coming?"

"Let's say he inherited his Aunt Teri's ability to present his case," Damon answered with a smile. "I just want to say hello to Ahmad, then I'll come help you in the kitchen."

Maxine was in her state of perpetual kitchen motion when Damon walked back in.

"I'm so glad you're here." She smiled, stopped for a minute, and gave him a hug. "How are you?"

"A little tired, but well. Did Teri tell you about my WNBA project?"

"No. What are you doing for the WNBA?"

"It's an endorsement deal. Concerts in every city where there's a WNBA franchise."

"That's fabulous, Damon." She took a pan of corn bread out of the oven and began cutting it into squares. "But Chicago doesn't have a WNBA team."

"That's true, but it's not a problem. We'll just arrange for you to go see a concert in a city of your choice. We have an airline sponsor."

"You're kidding?"

"It's my birthday gift to Ahmad." Damon tried not to look at the door every time someone arrived.

"He's going to love you forever for that." Maxine found herself watching the door, too. "Damon, where's Teri?"

"She was up at Moore, Freeman earlier. I haven't seen her since."

"Is she looking for a job?"

"I don't know. You're going to have to ask Teri."

It was as if she heard her name. Teri arrived looking wonderful, like a breath of fresh air. No one could have guessed she had made her transformation in a dressing room at the mall. Ahmad was the first to greet her.

"Aunt Teri, you look really nice." He kissed her on the cheek.

"Thank you, sweetie. Happy birthday." She kissed

him back and handed him the shopping bag with his gifts.

She put on her game face and headed toward the living room before Ahmad could ask her why she and Damon hadn't arrived together. He was a big fan of Damon's. *Hell, everyone in my family is a big fan of Damon's.*

"Good evening, everyone."

"Hey, Teri. I like those shoes, girl. When did you get them?" Bird was probably more familiar with Teri's closet than she was herself.

"Yeah, I like that dress, too," Maxine added. She pulled Teri into the kitchen.

"Where have you been all day?"

"I went shopping."

"But why did you turn off your cell phone?"

"I needed some time to think and clear my head."

"What happened at Moore, Freeman? Are you looking for a job?"

"Moore, Freeman? How did you know I was there?" She knew the answer already. She looked at Damon, who was talking with Bird and Lem. "Why is he here?"

"Because it's Ahmad's birthday and he wanted him here, and because I invited him."

"Why did you do that?"

"Teri, no one has time to check and see if you and Damon are having an off day, which you apparently are. You really need to get over yourself."

"Get *over* myself?"

"Yes. You always make everything about you. Whatever goes on between you guys is your business, not ours."

"Well, if that were really true, why are you and Bird always trying to get in my business?"

"Busted." Maxine put her arms around her older sister. "Because we care about you. We can't help it . . . the meddling or the caring. So just get over it. You're stuck with us."

When the family and Ahmad's friends crowded into the Chadways' small dining room everyone gasped at the spread in front of them. The dining room table for six was covered with wonderful dishes Maxine had lovingly prepared in honor of the birth of her firstborn.

Kenny looked around at everyone and grinned. "Y'all ready to eat?"

"Kenny, stop playing and bless the food," Bird demanded. "You know we're hungry."

"Teri, have some cake." Maxine offered after everyone had serenaded Ahmad with the birthday song.

"No, thank you. I really couldn't eat another bite."

"Your sister made a great chocolate cake." Damon smiled at her.

"I said I'm not hungry." Her response was cool, even though she managed to smile. "But I will take a slice home." She stood up, and Maxine stood, too.

"I'll get the aluminum foil. You stay and visit."

Teri couldn't think of one thing she wanted to say to anyone except to Damon, and that wouldn't be in front of her family.

"Well, people, it's been great, but I have an early flight in the morning so unfortunately I have to go." Damon stood up from the table.

"Where you headed, man?" Lem licked the chocolate frosting off his fork.

"Los Angeles."

"Need me to hook you up with a haircut before you jet?" Bird eyed his head.

"I've got a five A.M. flight to the coast, Bird. You gonna meet me at Cut It Up around two?"

"Hell, no," Lem answered for her and everyone laughed. "Bird doesn't know what two A.M. looks like."

The family continued laughing. Maxine handed Damon the cake she'd cut for Teri, since he was leaving first and she knew how much he loved her chocolate cake. She gave him a kiss on the cheek before he left the dining room. "Have a safe trip."

"I know, you're going with him," Bird said to Teri before Damon was out of the house. "It's not like you're stuck in Chicago. Maxine and I can handle the store while you're away."

"Go to L.A. with Damon?" Teri shook her head. "I have too much work at the store." No matter what she said, it wouldn't be a right answer and she wasn't ready to get into what had gone on between them.

seventeen

teri drove home so fast she made it there before Damon. She was sitting in the living room on the sofa when he walked in the door. Damon looked surprised to see her sitting there, and uncertain. She looked at him, handsome as ever in a green sweater and black pants, and felt her emotions stirring. She got up and went into the kitchen for some juice. *I'm not having any more panic attacks today, not over him,* she promised herself.

He was sitting on the sofa when she returned, and she sat beside him.

"I guess you want to talk to me," he began.

"Why would you think that?"

"Because you came to my office. My secretary informed me that you were there to see me. You were sitting in my office waiting for me."

"If you recall, I used to be a partner at Moore, Freeman. I stopped by to speak with a few of the partners." She kicked off her shoes. New shoes, like a good man, always hurt a little until they were properly broken in.

"You were there to speak to the partners? About what?"

"I've been thinking about going back to law. My work at the store is just about complete and it's time I started looking for a job again."

"But why would you talk to them? And I thought you were going to help me with my WNBA project."

"When I attempted to speak to you about that, you weren't interested, so I've moved on." Her tone was extremely cool.

"Oh, Teri, please. You are so full of crap. What is all this really about?"

"What is all *what* really about?" She appeared amused.

"Last night I thought we were having a relationship, until you informed me we weren't."

"I never said that," she cut in.

"I believe I was talking." He looked at her and she could tell he was angry. "You said you didn't want a relationship."

"I never said that."

"Well, you never said you did."

It seemed like forever when he started talking again. "Then I get a message from my secretary that you're in my office waiting, and by the time I get there you practically knock me down as you get on the elevator and then pretend that you didn't see me."

"I didn't," she lied.

"Teri, you looked me right in the eye."

"My mind must have been somewhere else."

"What is it? Araina? Is that what this is about?"

"Who's Araina?"

"The young lady I got off the elevator with, the very pretty one. Did you happen to notice her?"

"Chicago is full of very pretty women."

"Okay, whatever. . . . But what about tonight at Ahmad's party? You barely spoke to me. What's going on?"

"It was Ahmad's party. His night. You stole the show when you gave him a trip to one of your basketball concerts. Do you always need all the attention?"

"What?" She sounded like a crazy woman to him. "Who are you, and what have you done with Teri Joseph?"

"Who am I?" A puzzled look covered her face.

"Yes. Because I know Teri Joseph pretty well, and I'm obviously not talking to her. So who the hell are you?"

"Damon, please. You think you know me, but you really don't."

"I'm starting to believe that." He was clearly frustrated and she was enjoying herself. She liked seeing him squirm for once.

"Maxine said she had been trying to reach you all day and you never came in to the store."

"That's because I had some other appointments."

"And you didn't bother telling her? Come on, you guys tell each other everything."

"See, Damon Carter, you're wrong. We don't tell each other everything, and you don't know as much as you think you know."

"I know this much. You're not being honest and you're hiding something. What, I don't know, but I really don't have time to play games with you and try to figure it out."

"I'm not hiding anything from you, Damon." If he wasn't going to be man enough and tell her he was moving out of her house, she certainly wasn't going to let him know that she'd seen his newspaper with the circled ads.

"You're hiding something. And your sisters think I know what it is. Do you know about the ads?"

"What ads?" Teri almost dropped her glass. *He does know I was in his office!*

Damon noticed the change immediately and wondered why Maxine's ads with the radio station had her so upset. There were things about Teri that annoyed him, as with any person. But he couldn't believe she was jealous that Maxine had temporarily taken the spotlight, especially when she'd always been so supportive of her sisters.

"The ads Maxine recorded with J.B. and Justine at the radio station this afternoon. She would have told you if you had spoken to her."

"I did speak to her. I forgot about those." She sighed with relief and looked at him thoughtfully.

"All right, Teri. I give up. Is there anything you'd like to talk about?"

"No. Is there anything you'd like to talk about?"

"I've said what I have to say. I've got a very early flight."

"I heard. How long are you going to be gone?"

"I'm not sure. I wanted to be here for Thanksgiving, but I might just stay in L.A. and visit friends, or kick it in San Francisco."

"You're not going to be here for Thanksgiving? Did you tell my family that?"

"No, why?"

"You know how they feel about you. They wouldn't like it if you weren't around for Thanksgiving, especially with the store reopening and the big dinner for the homeless. We could really use your help."

"I very much wanted to be there and I really enjoy being around your family."

"So, what's the problem?"

"I also know how you feel about me having a relationship with your family when we aren't having one."

"That's never stopped you before." She looked at him sideways.

"Yes, but I'm a little tired of being in uncomfortable situations with you. Thanksgiving is a special family holiday, and I don't want you to be uncomfortable or me, so I'm just going to spend some time in California with my brother and some friends. I think that would be best for all parties concerned. Don't you?"

Teri couldn't believe what she was hearing. She never thought he would listen to her and not come around her family, especially now. Completely at a loss for words, she sat there staring at him like he had two heads.

Her silence made him uncomfortable, as usual, and he was tired of it.

"I see you're in agreement, so I'm gonna say good night."

He disappeared up the stairs in a matter of seconds.

"Now I've really gone and done it. Instead of making things right, I'm making them worse," Teri whispered to herself. "I knew I would mess it up." *That's why my other marriages failed. It's me, not them.* Tears sprung to her eyes.

"No," she whispered fiercely. "No crying."

She saw the slice of birthday cake Maxine had wrapped up for Damon sitting on the coffee table. In her hasty departure, she had neglected to bring home another slice for herself. She could smell Maxine's double-double fudge frosting. She pulled off the aluminum foil and inhaled the heavenly scent of chocolate before she ran a finger across the foil to remove the frosting that had stuck to it.

This is wonderful. She closed her eyes and sighed as the sweetness melted on her tongue.

She didn't even go into the kitchen for a fork. She ate the triple-layered cake with her fingers and licked them clean.

"That was so good."

Who was it that said chocolate was as good as sex? They said it sends an orgasmic-like sensation to the brain. Is that why they always show women eating gallons of chocolate ice cream in the movies when they have man problems? Hmmm. I know I could have eaten the entire cake if it was in front of me.

Damon drove his car to his father's house very early the next morning and parked it inside the garage. The temperature had plummeted and every Chicagoan knew snow would soon be in the forecast. He didn't want his car exposed to the elements, sitting in Teri's driveway while he was away.

An airport shuttle delivered him to the terminal in ample time. Once inside, he grabbed a newspaper, a couple of cinnamon rolls, and a carton of milk before boarding the aircraft. He was asleep before the plane taxied out to the runway.

Maxine and Bird phoned Teri early that morning on a three-way call.

"All right, girl, dish. What's up with the new

shoes and dress? Were you dressing up for Damon?" Bird's laughter could be infectious.

Teri was barely awake. Yesterday's drama had worn her out and she would have loved to spend the day in bed regrouping, especially with Damon out of town and out of her house.

"Who said I was wearing new shoes and a new dress?" She yawned.

"Please, Teri. We know what's in your closet." Bird wasn't about to let up. "And why did you turn off your cell phone and avoid Maxine all day?"

"I was trying to avoid everyone. I just needed some time to think."

"Teri, what's really going on? Is there something you want to tell us?" Maxine's voice was soothing.

"Damon's on his way to Los Angeles. Now you know as much as I do."

"I didn't ask about Damon. I asked about you."

"Yeah, T. We just want to know if you're okay. We're not trying to be all up in your and Damon's business," Bird finished softly.

"I'm fine, you guys, really I am. Now I have to go. I'll see you at the store, Maxine." She clicked off the line.

"She's lying," Bird surmised.

"I know," Maxine agreed. "But we need to leave her alone. She'll tell us when she wants us to know."

* * *

Damon woke up somewhere west of the Mississippi. He stretched and opened up his newspaper, but his thoughts kept taking him to Teri. He flipped through it until he got to the real estate section, and ran yesterday's events through his mind as he glanced through the apartments available.

Suddenly, he sat straight up in his seat. He got his briefcase down from the overhead baggage compartment and pulled out a stack of magazines and the real estate section from yesterday's newspaper.

He looked at the circles covering the page. He had gone through the listings first thing yesterday morning out of frustration. He had found several things he liked and was on his way to leave a deposit on one, but Araina had advised him to talk to Teri before he did anything drastic like moving out. Damon was glad he had listened when he learned that she was waiting in his office.

He would have to confront her about his suspicion in person, and that wouldn't be possible for at least a week. They could never discuss something as sensitive as this over the phone. *Damn.* He felt hemmed in and helpless more than thirty-five thousand feet above the earth. He closed his eyes and silently prayed.

eighteen

Teri was prepared for anything when she arrived at the store that morning, even one of Bird's unannounced entrances. Maxine was overseeing the restocking of the shelves with canned goods and packaged nonperishable items.

Teri hadn't really had the time to look at the store before, but today she could really see the progress. They had put the store back together even better than she remembered. She looked around at all the improvements and smiled. Seeing the place revived so beautifully made her day. *Daddy would be so proud.*

"Good morning." Maxine smiled at Teri as she passed by.

"It really looks great in here." Teri smiled excitedly. "Like a real store again."

"It looks better." Maxine was equally pleased with what had been accomplished. "All the food will be on the shelves by the day before Thanksgiving. We'll set up the food for the dinner in the produce area, and put the produce in place early Friday morning."

"Maxine, you didn't find a place to hold the dinner yet?" Teri went into the office and Maxine followed her.

"No."

"Why not?"

"Because we're having it here."

"Maxine, how can we? There's not enough room."

"It'll be fine, Teri. Look, I never got a chance to tell you about the interviews they want us to do Thanksgiving Eve, so keep your calendar free. You, Bird and myself are going to start off on the Morning Show with Justine and J.B."

"You're kidding?"

"No."

"That's great news."

"That's what I was trying to tell you yesterday."

Teri's mind shifted to Damon momentarily. "I know. Are you sure there's enough food and space for everyone to eat? With all this radio promotion, we're going to attract a lot of people. I just don't want this thing to backfire on us and turn into a disaster."

"A disaster?" Maxine laughed at the thought. "Everything's under control."

"Maybe it's my life that's a disaster." Teri flopped in the chair behind her desk and looked up at Maxine.

"What happened?"

Teri shook her head, trying to fight back the same tears she had fought with the night before.

"Teri . . . what is it?" Maxine reached for her sister's hand.

"I don't want to get into all of that now, but Damon's going to be moving out when he returns from California."

"Teri, no . . . what happened?"

"It's a long story. But I want you guys to still be friends with him. He needs you, and you guys obviously need him. I've been so selfish." She quickly brushed a tear from the corner of her eye.

"So . . . what are you going to do now that the store is finished?" Maxine changed the subject. "I know you've got something lined up."

"I was supposed to work on Damon's WNBA project with him, but I sort of messed that up." Teri managed a feeble smile.

"Kenny wants me to come back and help him at Chadway Towing."

"You're kidding? What did you say?"

"I asked him if he was going to pay me a salary."

"Maxine, you didn't?" Teri had to laugh.

"I sure did."

"So, what are you going to do?"

"I haven't made a decision yet."

"What do you want to do?"

"It might be nice to be back at Chadway." She

was practically blushing. "But I love this store. I've been thinking about running it, at least until we hire someone else, if it's okay with everyone."

"Maxine, I think that's a wonderful idea. You'd be perfect."

"Do you really think so?"

"Yes. I couldn't think of anyone more perfect. But what about Kenny? You just said he asked you to work at the garage."

"Chadway is his baby. I'll talk it over with him, now that you've approved. And it's just temporary."

"But it could become permanent," Teri pointed out.

"We'll see what happens."

"Kenny can be stubborn."

"Yeah, just like you and Bird."

"Bird isn't stubborn." Teri laughed. "She's just spoiled."

"Whatever. I'll deal with Kenny. He'll get over himself."

"Are we talking about the same Kenny Chadway?" Teri laughed again.

"You're feeling better." Maxine sounded pleased.

"I should have told you about Damon moving out last night. You know I act like a crazy woman when I try to keep things in."

"That's the understatement of the year."

"I'm having lunch with my old friend Brian today, to see what's going on in the world of law."

"Is that why you were at Moore, Freeman yesterday?" Maxine asked.

"No," Teri answered softly.

"So, why were you there?"

"Not today." Teri looked at her sister and Maxine could see she was still hurting, despite the laughter. "I'll tell you, but not today."

Maxine eyed Teri carefully as she bent over her paperwork and wondered what else had happened between her and Damon. He was on a plane on his way to California, and she was in Chicago on the verge of tears.

Kenny and Lem sat down together in his office for lunch. Maxine had packed enough leftovers for them both, and they were having a feast. Containers of everything they had eaten the night before covered Kenny's desk. There was a big piece of chocolate cake in the center.

"Now, this is what I call lunch." Kenny chewed happily, like a little boy. Lem placed several cans of grape soda on the table and picked up his plate.

"Ahmad's birthday party was really nice." Lem dug into the collards they had heated in the microwave along with the rest of the food. It had been a process but definitely worth the wait.

"Even old Damon was there." Lem grinned. "Did you sense a little tension there?"

"Yes, when he said he was going to California.

You know how Teri likes to run things. He probably didn't ask her permission." Kenny laughed.

"Man, you're wrong, but you're probably right. We need to invite him out for a night on the town and school him on how to live with a Joseph woman." Lem laughed.

"Yeah, but it looks like he's hanging in there on his own. Think those two will ever get married?"

"If Bird has anything to do with it, they will."

"Big Bird . . . flapping her wings again." Kenny grinned.

"She ain't goin' nowhere."

"Except to Lake Shore Drive." Kenny laughed.

"Oh, so you got jokes today. . . . Was last night the first time you had the entire family in your house for dinner?"

"Yeah, man. I never noticed how small the place was, until all of you were in there last night. It was great, but we could use a little more room."

"Now, can't you see you and Maxine doing that at Mama Joe's house?"

Kenny was silent for a long time. Lem finished his lunch and cut off a big slice of cake.

"Yeah, I can see it," Kenny finally said.

"And?"

"And what?" Kenny took the rest of the cake.

"And what are you going to do about it?"

"I'll talk to Teri on Sunday, over dinner at Mama Joe's house."

* * *

Teri was engrossed in a novel when Brian arrived at their favorite Indian restaurant for lunch. It wasn't far from Green, Norris and it was a haunt for many of the lawyers who worked in the area, so, she'd dressed accordingly in perfect corporate attire.

"How are you, Teri?" Brian slid into the seat across from her.

She was so into the book, he startled her. "Brian, don't sneak up on me like that."

"You just didn't notice me because you were deep into the story."

Teri smiled and closed the book. "I've forgotten how much I enjoyed reading for pleasure. I'm usually so busy with work, I never have enough time for anything except the newspaper."

"And you're ready to come back. Why?"

"Old habits are hard to break."

They decided on the buffet and chose tandoori chicken, saffron rice, and curried vegetables. A waiter brought them fresh, hot naan bread.

"I thought you were working at your family's grocery store."

"That project is just about complete. We open on Thanksgiving." She frowned and shook her head.

"What's wrong?"

"Maxine had an idea to put together a wonderful dinner for the homeless and for people who just don't have enough money for dinner."

"That's a fabulous idea."

"It was, until the entire thing snowballed into an invitation for the entire city. Maxine got the most popular radio station in the city to promote the dinner."

"That's wonderful."

"It is, except we don't have a place to feed everyone. I told her to find a church, but she won't budge."

"You'll think of something, Teri Joseph. You always do."

nineteen

teri lay in bed staring at the telephone, willing it to ring. She picked up a book on relationships that she had purchased right after lunch with Brian. But as hard as she tried, she couldn't concentrate. She found herself constantly revisiting their conversations, dancing in the kitchen, and every other wonderful thing that she and Damon had done together since he moved into the house. She moaned and covered her head with a pillow.

Kenny came home early from work that night. Maxine had a million things on her mind when she walked in the door with her briefcase and usual stack of folders.

"For you, madam." He was waiting in the kitchen with a bottle of champagne. He took her things and placed them on the table, then led her to a chair.

Maxine was speechless. She looked at the champagne and then at him. "Thanks, Kenny." The words came from somewhere.

"You are so very welcome." He sat across from her, took her shoes off, and began to massage her feet.

"Kenny, what is this about?" His strong hands felt so good massaging her feet.

"This is about me loving and appreciating my wife." He continued the foot massage.

She knew her husband too well but remained silent, enjoying the foot massage.

"Maxine, let's go to a movie tonight," he suggested.

"A movie?" The idea of a night out with her husband was intriguing. "Kenny Chadway, what's going on here?"

"I had a rough day, and I just want to take my wife out and spend some time with her alone."

"Is that all?" She couldn't help wondering if this had something to do with moving into Mama Joe's house. Neither of them had mentioned it since that fateful Sunday dinner.

She eyed him carefully. "All right, Kenny, let's go."

Bird heated up the leftovers from the Thai food lunch she had shared with Teri. It was late Friday night and she had another big day at the salon tomorrow. Friday and Saturday were her busiest days at Cut It Up. She was glad she had the leftovers. She had come straight home from work and heated them up while Lem washed up the baby and read him a story.

"What's all this?" He took a seat at the dining room table.

"Thai food." She picked up some of the noodles with a pair of chopsticks.

"I thought we were going to cut back on eating out so we can save money for the condo?"

"We don't have a condo, remember? And Teri bought the food."

"Teri?"

"We had lunch yesterday, and these were the left-overs."

"The Van Adams aren't a charity case."

"Nobody said we were, Lem. It's just a few left-overs. And I'm too tired for this tonight."

"Okay, baby. I'm sorry. I just want to be the man of our family."

"You are the man."

"Well, maybe I'll feel more like the man of this house when you stop running to your sister every time something goes wrong. You never give me a chance to handle it."

"All right, I'll let you handle it. I suppose you've got a magic credit fixer or financing?"

Teri looked at the phone again and wanted so badly to call Damon, if only to see if he had arrived in Los

Angeles safely. But she hadn't heard of any plane crashes on the news, so she knew he was there. She went into the kitchen for a cup of tea. *Why is life so hard, or why do I make it so hard?*

Maxine and Kenny were smiling when they entered the restored old movie theater. The owner had refurbished it with red velvet curtains, modern swivel chairs, and stadium seating. The theater was known for its double features. The selections for the evening were *Brown Sugar* and *Set It Off*.

"This is perfect, Kenny. I've been wanting to see this movie and I love *Set It Off*."

"Ain't nothin' like watching four serious sisters rob a bank."

Maxine laughed happily as they were served chili dogs, chili cheese fries, and cherry Cokes. "Kenny, thanks for bringing me here." She happily planted a kiss on his lips.

"Thanks for coming." He grinned.

"You know I'd go anywhere with you. You're my dance partner for life."

"I always want you to be happy, baby," Lem said.

He and Bird were curled up on the sofa watching television with Jay between them.

"I am happy." She kissed him and rubbed his head. "Why would you think I wasn't?"

"I know how badly you want to move, and—"

"Lem, I don't need a Lake Shore Drive condominium to make me happy. What makes me happy is you."

"But what if we lose our ten thousand dollars?"

"I am not losing my ten thousand dollars." Bird was serious. "And no matter what, we'll always have each other."

"Yeah, but we may not have a place to live."

"Why?"

"I told you I was going to talk to Kenny and I did. He's agreed to move into Mama Joe's house," Lem said.

"He did? I never thought he would do that."

"Then what did you think was going to happen?"

"I don't know. I figured things would just kind of work themselves out." She looked up at him with puppy dog eyes.

"Remember that night I asked you if you were sure you wanted to move?"

"Yes . . . but I changed my mind since all the drama."

"Baby, life is full of drama, and we can't change our minds every time some comes our way. This isn't just about us anymore. It's about Maxine and Kenny wanting to move in here now."

"Well, none of us may be moving anywhere until we talk to Teri."

* * *

Maxine and Kenny walked out of the theater holding hands.

"I'm going to have to purchase those movies on DVD." Kenny smiled.

"Baby, we don't own a DVD player."

"We will when I set up our screening room."

"Screening room?" Maxine laughed. "We don't have enough room for that big screen TV you've been wanting to buy."

"We will when we move into Mama Joe's house."

"Move? Kenny, are you serious?"

"More than ever."

She covered her mouth and screamed.

"Bird's agreed to sell us her share of the house. All we need is Teri's."

The smile faded from Maxine's face. "I already asked her, and she said no."

"What?"

"She said no."

They walked to the car in silence.

"Did she say why?"

"She said it's the only tangible thing that still connects her to Daddy."

"Damn . . ."

"But you were going to do it for me, and that means a lot." She leaned over and kissed him.

"But I wanted you to have the house."

"We already have a house." She spoke softly.

"But we could use a bigger house." He was clearly disappointed.

"We'll get one." She took a deep breath. "Honey . . . would you mind if I managed J&H? It's temporary," she added quickly. "We've started interviews, but we haven't found the right person yet."

"Sure, baby. You ran Chadway well. You'll do a great job—so great, you and Teri will never find anyone to measure up."

"Yes, we will." She laughed and looked up at Kenny, who planted a kiss on her forehead. "Thank you, sweetie. Thanks for everything. You don't know how much your support means to me."

twenty

Teri was on her way out of the house to the gym when she ran smack into Maxine. She was so preoccupied that she hadn't noticed that her sister was standing behind her while she was locking the front door, until she turned around and practically ran her over.

"Maxine."

"Teri."

They stood looking at each other until Maxine laughed.

"When did you get here?" Teri laughed, too.

"While you were locking the door."

"But I didn't even hear you."

"Obviously. What's on your mind?"

"Everything, but I'm running late for my dance class. Can we talk later?"

"I was hoping we could have breakfast together. Kenny said I could manage the store," she declared excitedly.

"Kenny Chadway?" Teri paused to be sure of what she had heard.

"Yes."

"I don't know what to say about that."

"Then don't say anything." Maxine laughed happily. "We're not having Sunday dinner tomorrow, since we've all been so crazy with preparations for the store opening, but we do need to have a family meeting. Bird suggested drinks and appetizers around four."

"That's fine," Teri said as she got into the car. "Where are you headed?"

"I'm on my way to the shop. Bird's doing something different with my hair and I can't wait to see what she comes up with."

"She's the best."

"Did Damon call?"

"No, not yet. I've got to go," Teri yelled as she closed the window and sped down the street. "And why would I even expect him to?" She was talking to herself more often since he had left. She really missed having him to talk to.

Maxine sat at Bird's station, playing with her braids while her sister bid her last customer farewell. She had been so busy with J&H that she had just been tying her hair up with a scarf lately and barely noticed the new growth. Now, with her braids down and the scarf off, she was glad her sister had summoned her into the shop.

"Every time I sit in this chair, I thank God for a sister who's a hairdresser," she told Bird.

"And I had to beg you to come in here. So, what are we going to do with this stuff?" Bird's hand sifted through her braids, then she took out a pair of scissors and began cutting off the extensions

"You never told me what you were going to do." Maxine twisted around in the chair so she could see Bird.

"Girl, if you don't sit still, I'm gonna have to shave your head like Damon's." Bird laughed.

"I don't think I'm ready to try that look."

"So have you talked to Teri?" Bird asked.

"Yeah . . ."

"Is she upset Damon went to California?"

"I don't think so."

"Then what's her problem?"

"I don't know. I guess she's been hurt too many times. She's afraid to take a chance." Maxine's face was thoughtful.

"Maybe. But everyone's been hurt, and everybody's played the fool at one time or another."

"I know, but with Teri it's different. It's like something she said Dr. Pruit told her."

"What's that?"

"He said Teri equates love with her accomplishments, so she has a fear of failure."

"But everyone's afraid of a relationship failing and getting hurt."

"But Teri's not everyone. She needs to know that she doesn't have to earn love, that she's capable of being loved the way she is."

Bird sighed heavily. "Russell and Miles certainly didn't help the situation."

"No, they didn't."

"And I know Damon cheated, but he loves her."

Maxine frowned. "You know that and I know that, and I'm pretty sure Damon knows it, too. Teri's the one who needs to be convinced."

Damon got in his rented luxury sedan and drove west on Olympic, away from the Staples Center, where he had just outlined the specifics of the concert with the Sparks. They had just completed their first season in the building, and management was very interested in promoting games to increase attendance.

He had to smile at the car that was so not him. He would have preferred something less flashy, but he was in the land of stars and cars, and it was a necessary tool for business in Los Angeles.

It was a beautiful, extremely warm day in southern California. He stretched and opened the sun roof. The sun felt good, especially after all the nasty weather in Chicago.

He was very familiar with the city and he drove until he got to Beverly Hills. He found a parking lot on Rodeo Drive, left his car with the attendant, and started walking. He walked in and out of the numerous famous stores and paused as two gorgeous, model-like women gave him the eye. He turned around to look as they strutted by and laughed. *I feel like Eddie Murphy in* Beverly Hills Cop. He smiled and continued walking, admiring the California babes who cast him sensual glances. *Damn. L.A. sure has some fine women.*

He found himself in front of an exclusive jewelry store and went inside. He couldn't help thinking of Teri when he saw the brilliantly cut diamonds.

"May I help you?" A saleslady smiled. "With anything?" she suggestively added.

"No, thanks." He smiled. "But I'll be sure to let you know if you can."

He walked through the store, admiring the selection of magnificent engagement rings in various settings, as well as earrings, necklaces, and bracelets.

"Would you like me to show you something?" the same lady asked.

"I would like to see that one, please." He surprised himself when he pointed out a three-carat diamond engagement ring surrounded by a cluster of smaller stones.

"Your taste is exquisite." The woman smiled. "Lucky lady." She placed the ring in a blue velvet box on the counter.

Damon picked the ring up and smiled. Then he returned the ring to the box. "Thank you."

The lady handed him a business card. "Just in case you may need some help with anything else."

Maxine sat in the chair, admiring her newly twisted do. "You've done it again, Bird." She smiled and smiled. "Got me all hooked up in time for the store opening."

"I wanted to get you in here before your big debut, so I could redo it if you didn't like it." She took the mirror from her sister and returned it to the counter, while Maxine put on a pair of earrings.

"There may not be a dinner."

"No dinner? That's all everyone is talking about. Don't we have enough food?"

"We have plenty of food."

"Then what's the problem?"

"Teri doesn't think we should have it at the store."

"Why not?"

"Because with all of the radio spots and publicity, she says it's out of control. She said there's going to be too many people and we can't feed them all in the store."

"So, what are we supposed to do with all the food that's already been donated?"

"She wants me to find a church for the dinner."

"No way . . . we're having dinner at the store."

Maxine got a broom and swept the floor, while

Bird put away the tools from her station. Maxine hummed softly and smiled while she swept.

Bird watched her dump the debris in a wastebasket. "What's got you in such a good mood?"

"Kenny and I went out on a date last night."

"Dish, girl. I've been waiting on Teri and Damon to get busy, and you're the one making all the power moves."

"We only went to the movies . . . but to the expensive one that's like a real theater."

"I've been trying to get Lem to take me. We've been waiting until there was something we really wanted to see."

"We saw *Brown Sugar.*" Maxine grinned.

"I'm so glad you two are back together. I really felt bad after you guys got into it over the house."

"He surprised me last night. He said we, the Chadways, could move into Mama Joe's house. He said he had talked to Lem and you agreed to sell me your share."

"I did. So now you have two thirds . . ."

"I know what you're going to say, and I already asked her, and she said no."

"She did? I can't believe her." Bird looked determined. "When did you ask her?"

"The day after you first brought it up."

"Well, we're gonna ask her again . . . all of us."

"Slow down, little sister. I've already got that handled. We're having a family meeting."

"When?"

"Tomorrow at four, at your place, and you're making appetizers and drinks."

"I am?"

"Yes, Miss Lake Shore Drive."

"Appetizers?"

"Girl, just go to the gourmet shop and get something frozen that you can heat up. And don't burn them." She waved a warning finger in her younger sister's face before she took out several twenties and tucked them in Bird's appointment book.

"Okay." Bird laughed as she tucked the bills into a bank deposit envelope. "I hope they have something I can't annihilate."

Maxine laughed at the thought, then grew serious. "Bird, no matter what happens, I really appreciate what you did. And I am truly amazed by Kenny. I still can't believe he's doing this for me."

"That's special, Maxine."

"I just hope Teri doesn't think we're ganging up on her. We're not, are we?"

"No. It's a family meeting and we need to discuss the dinner now, too."

"Sounds good." Maxine reached out and hugged her sister tightly. "Thanks, Bird. I love you."

"I love you, too. See you tomorrow." She watched Maxine's hips swing as she walked out of the shop with her freshly twisted coif, and couldn't remember when she thought her sister looked more beautiful.

twenty-one

It was raining again on Sunday. Teri was tempted to stay home from church and camp out in front of the fireplace with the big screen TV, but she didn't. "Sunday is the Lord's Day," she could hear her mother say. "You always want to give Him the first day of the week." As children, they were never allowed to do anything or go anywhere until after they had attended church.

Maxine looked at the pouring rain and frowned. It was getting close to Thanksgiving, and the Weather Channel had predicted rain over the next week. *Maybe Teri is right about the dinner. If the dinner ends up getting cancelled, that will really make the family look bad.* She shuddered at the thought.

"Look at you, looking all good and smelling all good." Kenny walked up behind her and pulled her into his arms. "I like your new hairdo. Big Bird showed out." He fingered one of the twists and pulled her closer.

"She did, didn't she?"

They stood looking out of the window together at the downpour.

"I know what you're thinking."

"Okay . . . what am I thinking, Mr. Chadway?"

"It's gonna rain on your big dinner. But I don't want you worrying your pretty head, so I put in an extra word with the Man upstairs this morning, and asked him not to let it rain on Thanksgiving."

"You did?" She turned to look at him and smiled. He had picked the right moment to be supportive.

"I sure did." He grinned.

"Thanks, baby." But the family meeting they were all about to attend still concerned her.

Bird reread the directions on the boxes for frozen egg rolls and shrimp, to make sure she had the oven set at the correct temperature. She was known for burning things, but she didn't want her appetizers undercooked and frozen in the center, either.

"Baby, get the pop out of the fridge and get some ice for me, please." She smiled at Lem.

There had been no further discussion about the loan, although Lem had started to bring in moving boxes and tape.

The timer on the oven rang and the doorbell

right behind it. Teri came into the kitchen, carrying pastry boxes from their favorite bakery.

"Looks like somebody's moving around here." She sat the boxes on the table.

"Moving up and out." Lem poured ice into a cooler and Bird tried not to fidget.

"So everything's fine?" Teri looked at Bird and then Lem.

"Fine as wine in the summertime." He met Teri's eye.

"Good." Teri smiled. "Can I help with anything?"

"We've got everything under control." Lem smiled. "Why don't you just take a seat and talk to your nephew?"

"Okay." She left the kitchen and went into the living room with the baby.

"Lem," Bird whispered sharply. "Cut it out."

"What?"

"You know what."

"She can't even come in the house without trying to take over," he whispered loudly.

"She doesn't mean to. She's just used to being the big sister."

"Well, it's time for big sister to recognize that baby sister has a man to help her out now."

The doorbell rang and Teri opened the door for the Chadways. While they were hugging and kissing, Bird brought in her appetizers and Lem followed with the drinks.

"Hey, everybody." Maxine sent the girls and Jay up to her old bedroom to play. Ahmad disappeared into the kitchen, so he was out of sight but still able to hear what the adults were discussing.

Teri placed a few of the shrimp on her plate and sprinkled them with hot sauce. She bit into one and was surprised by how tasty it was. "These are good, Bird." She helped herself to a few more and added an egg roll. "Okay, so what's this meeting all about?"

The Chadways and Van Adamses looked at one another.

"We want to talk about the house, Teri," Maxine started.

"And the dinner at the store," Bird added.

"The last time we had dinner, we were discussing what to do with the house when Bird and Lem move out." Maxine took a sip of her drink.

"I remember. Bird suggested that you and Kenny move in, and I agreed." Teri grabbed a can of pop and a glass of ice. "But you were against that idea, weren't you, Kenny?"

Kenny looked at Maxine. "I was . . ."

"That's right," Maxine joined in, choosing her words carefully. "Well, Kenny and I have discussed it further, and we've agreed to move in."

"Wonderful," Teri said. "I think that's perfect." She looked around the dining room table. "Bird, I brought an Oreo cookie cheesecake. Where is it?"

"It's in the refrigerator. I'll go get it." She stood up, and Lem stood with her.

"I'll get it. You stay here," he told his wife.

"Is there more?" Teri looked at her sisters.

"Yes, there is." Maxine's serious but tentative tone arrested Teri's attention. "Kenny and I won't move in unless we're able to own the house. Bird's selling me her share and I have mine, so all we need is yours."

Lem walked back in the dining room with the cheesecake and an apple pie.

"Wait. . . . let me be sure I heard this correctly. You want me to sell you my share of the house?" A wild look crept into Teri's eyes and Bird took a deep breath.

"Yes." Maxine was cool as she spoke. "Kenny and I already own a house, and we're not going to sell a house and own nothing."

"No." Teri was almost too calm.

"Why not?" Maxine and Bird chorused while Kenny and Lem exchanged glances.

"Because I don't want to." Teri was clearly trying to remain calm.

"But why?" Bird asked softly. "You have a house. I'm willing to give up my share, and that way all of us will own property."

"No," Teri replied firmly.

"You won't have to come out of your pocket any-more for taxes and repairs. That'll be our responsibility now," Maxine added hoping something would change her sister's mind.

"No." Teri crossed her legs and folded her arms, and looked at her sisters.

"Teri, you're not being reasonable." Lem was in the conversation now.

"This is none of your business." She glared at Lem.

"Anything that affects my wife is my business," Lem quickly corrected. "Maybe if you had a husband, you would understand and stop trying to interfere in Bird's and my business all the time."

"Lem!" Bird was surprised by her husband's angry outburst.

"No, don't say anything to his silly, stupid ass," Teri said. "Lem, you're such a big man, you couldn't even qualify to get a loan to buy a house for your wife and child. So don't talk to me until you're able to step up to the plate. When I feel you're able to be the man, that's when I'll stop interfering in my little sister's life."

"You run off any man that's ever tried to be a part of your life," Lem fired back.

"All right." Maxine stood up. "That's not what we're here for. We're supposed to be a family."

"We're a family as long as Teri runs everything." Lem refused to back down.

"I've had enough of this." Teri stood up from the table.

"Wait, Teri." Kenny joined in the conversation. "Lem may not have chosen the correct words, but he was right when he said that what affects Bird and Maxine affects us. We are married."

A look of disgust covered Teri's face.

"What? You don't agree?" Kenny asked.

"No. My business with my sisters is my business, and I'm not selling my interest in the house to placate your little ego."

Kenny visibly paused to collect his thoughts. "Teri. I'm going to try and forget you said that and remind you that you're doing this for your sister, so don't make this all about me."

"Oh, please, Kenny. You're just as tired as Lem. Always wanting Maxine to do what you want. So save the speeches. At least Lem cares about his wife enough to support Bird in the things she wants to do."

Kenny was speechless. He was also embarrassed and angry.

"Who made you the judge?" he yelled back. "That's your problem: you want to run everything and everybody like a courtroom. You are so out of touch with reality. Whatever's been going on with Maxine and me is our business. That's the one thing you seem to have a problem with . . . minding your own business. But then, maybe that's because you don't have any business but *bizness,* if you get my drift. You can't deal with your sisters' husbands, because now you can't boss Maxine and Bird around and run their lives the way you want to. Somebody else has an opinion that isn't yours, and you don't want to hear it.

"But this is the real world, Teri, and it's time for you to get back in it. That's why you can't deal with Damon: you can't tell him what to do. You can't control him. He's obviously tired of your bullshit, or else he'd be here instead of across the country in California. You need to get a life, and then maybe you wouldn't be so determined to hold on to material things. Try holding on to a man for a change."

Teri remained seated and extremely quiet. She put a hand to her forehead and massaged her right temple.

Kenny was immediately sorry. He knew he had said too much, but it was too late. Everything had gone way out of control.

"Are you okay, Teri?" Maxine spoke softly.

She was not okay. She wanted to break down and cry . . . but she would never do that in front of all of them.

"I'm fine, Maxine." Her tone was cool and quiet but very much in control.

Ahmad couldn't believe what he was hearing. He wanted to run out of the kitchen and give his aunt a big hug. *And why is Damon in California? He should be here to have her back, the way Dad stood up for Mom, and Uncle Lem for Aunt Bird.*

"You're right Kenny, maybe I do need a life outside of this family. But whatever I have or don't have, I still own a third of this house. Maxine and Bird, you can do whatever you want with your shares. I'm not selling. It's one of the only things I have that my daddy gave me, and I'll never part with it."

Everyone was quiet as Teri gathered her things. "As far as the dinner, do what you want. Just don't ruin J&H and all Daddy did to make us proud."

She opened the door, walked out of the house, and closed it firmly behind her. No one moved, no one said anything. Maxine twisted her hair. Bird picked at a chipped fingernail, Lem moved cookie crumbs around his plate with a fork, and Kenny just rubbed his head. No one wanted things to go the way they had. It was supposed to be a simple family meeting . . . but things aren't always simple with families. No one had intended to hurt anyone's feelings. The Joseph sisters always had a deep unconditional love for one another, as well as their respective spouses. But when it comes to family, sometimes stuff just happens.

twenty-two

eri was amazed at how calm she was as she drove home. A lot had been said, maybe too much, and a retraction couldn't be made. If there was ever a time she needed Damon, it was now. He was the only person she felt comfortable enough with to confide in . . . especially something as personal as this. Maxine and Bird had always been her confidantes and best friends, but now she was feeling very much alone.

She took out her cell phone and looked at it. It was simply a matter of pressing one button, and she could talk to her best friend—but then, could she?

"That went really well," Bird finally said.

"I'm sorry, Maxine." Kenny was truly upset. "I never meant to say those things."

"I know, baby. But Teri said some things, too."

"Yeah, everybody said some things." Lem was still moving crumbs around with his fork. As much as he disliked Teri's intrusions into his and Bird's lives, he loved his sister-in-law.

"Lem . . ." Bird was standing over him. "Did you hear what I just said?"

"No, baby. I'm sorry, I didn't. I was thinking about Teri."

"Me, too." She slumped down in a chair beside him. "Everything is so messed up."

Ahmad was silent during the ride home with his parents. He was very concerned about his aunt. Should he ask his parents to take him by so he could spend the night? He closed his eyes so he could think.

Maxine glanced in the backseat and saw all three of her children asleep. Ahmad had been in the backyard shooting hoops when she and Bird cleaned up the kitchen, so she assumed he had been out there the entire time. No one had any idea that he had been in the kitchen listening.

"I hope Teri's okay." Maxine sighed.

"I don't see why she wouldn't be." Kenny managed to smile although his conscience was really eating him up. "Teri's tough. I wouldn't have gone there with her if she hadn't jumped all over me."

"I know, baby. She did say some pretty harsh things."

"How was I so blessed to have you for a wife and the mother of my children?"

"You just got it like that."

Ahmad had to smile when he heard his parents kissing. *But what are we gonna do about Aunt Teri? She's all alone.*

"I'm just concerned about Teri. You really hit a nerve when you brought up Damon. They've been having some sort of problems. The night of Ahmad's birthday dinner, I felt something was going on and I was hoping Damon would spill his guts, but he didn't say one word about anything to do with them. Teri's trained him well."

"So, how do you know they're having problems?"

"She told me. She wouldn't give me any details, but she said he's moving out."

Ahmad wanted to say something badly, but he knew his parents would kill him for getting in "grown folks' business."

"She forgot about Ahmad's birthday and then she disappeared for almost the entire day. She went up to Moore, Freeman and something happened. But all she told me was he's moving out."

"Damn, baby. I would have never said those things if I'd known all that." The guilt was overwhelming Kenny by now.

"No one really knew. I think she's been afraid of her feelings for him ever since they went out on a date to Groove Therapy."

"They went out on a date?"

"Yes."

"And Teri never told you anything?"

"She told me some, but I don't expect her to tell me everything, even if she is my sister."

"That's interesting."

Maxine looked determined. "Something happened between those two. I just know it."

"No doubt. I wonder what."

Teri turned on the water in her bathtub and poured in some of her favorite oil. She lit several scented candles and stepped into the water, enjoying its warmth as the water enveloped her. She settled back on her bath pillow with a glass of wine. It was time for a little introspection.

Whenever she thought about her exes she was immediately disgusted with herself.

But Damon is different, she heard a voice say from somewhere deep within.

I want to believe that so badly, but I'm afraid. Tears spilled out of her eyes and down her face. She slid down in the bathtub until her head was underwater, attempting to drown her thoughts and her tears.

Bird and Lem sat on the sofa with Jay in between them. Bird had read Jay a story, but it was one of those nights when he refused to go to sleep no matter what they tried.

"Jay, go to sleep, little boy." She kissed him on the head. He lay in Bird's lap and looked up at her and grinned.

She laughed and kissed him again. "See if you can get him to go to sleep, Lem. I'll go to the video store."

"Come here, little man." Lem grinned as he lifted his son out of Bird's lap. "Look at you, trying to give your mama a hard time."

Jay laughed as if he knew exactly what he was doing.

"Anything special you want to see?" Bird smiled when he tickled the baby.

"How about a DVD on what not to say to your sister-in-law?"

Bird sat down on the end of the sofa. "I feel bad about Teri, too. But she didn't have to go there with you or Kenny. That was wrong."

Lem kissed his son on the forehead. "I was wrong, too."

"She started it."

He paused before he continued speaking. "Baby, all I want is for you to come to me when you have a problem, and not Teri."

"I'm trying. It's just that she's always been there for me."

"I know. But I'm here now."

Ahmad looked at the clock and figured out the time in Los Angeles He picked up the telephone and dialed. The phone rang several times before it was answered.

"I know it's you, Ahmad." Damon laughed. "I've been expecting your call."

"You have?"

"Yes."

"Why?"

"Because you feel I haven't been doing my job. I know I promised you I would look after your aunt, and now I'm in California and I won't be back until after Thanksgiving."

"You won't?"

"No, man."

"Why?"

"Your auntie's kind of mad at me."

"Why? I know I'm not supposed to be in grown folks' business, but Mom said you're moving out of the house."

"I haven't told anyone I was moving."

"Well, Mom said you were moving out, and Aunt Teri is really upset and she wouldn't talk about it. Mom said Aunt Teri even forgot about my birthday dinner, and she couldn't find Aunt Teri the entire day."

"I had a hard time finding her that day, too."

"And now everyone's mad at Aunt Teri."

"Why?"

"Because Aunt Teri won't sell my mom and dad her share of Mama Joe's house. Everyone got into a really big fight tonight. You should have been there to stand up for her, the way Dad and Uncle Lem stood up for Mom and Aunt Bird."

"Ahmad, let me speak to Maxine."

"You can't."

"Why?"

"I was in the kitchen listening while they were fighting, and nobody knew it. Then I overheard Mom and Dad talking in the car on the way home. I think everyone really felt bad about Aunt Teri."

Damon was speechless. Ahmad had caught him in the car on his way to meet a friend for dinner, and he had to pull over to the side of the road so he could digest what he'd just heard. He sat there shaking his head. *I knew she saw that newspaper. Damn . . . she was in my office. That's why she ran out like that.*

Teri, Teri, Teri . . . why do you run away instead of talking to me? And then when you run, I run.

"Damon . . ."

"Huh?" He was a million miles away. "I'm sorry, Ahmad. I was just thinking about everything you told me."

"So, what are you going to do?"

Damon had to smile. Ahmad was an extremely intelligent, straight-up young man. You had to admire him, even when he *was* getting in "grown folks' business."

"I guess I won't be talking to Maxine."

"But what are you going to do?"

"I don't know what I can do."

"Don't you have a plan? You *are* coming back for Thanksgiving now, aren't you?"

"I don't know, Ahmad."

"But you have to come back for Thanksgiving. You have to be here for the store opening."

"I'd like to be there."

"So, why don't you come? Then you could see Aunt Teri."

"I have to think about all of this, Ahmad."

"What's there to think about? Aunt Teri needs you. And you're supposed to be around family for Thanksgiving. You're family."

Damon's head was spinning with all of the information Ahmad had given him.

"Tell you what, little man. I'll call you tomorrow and we'll figure something out."

Damon drove toward Beverly Hills, where he was having dinner. *Ahmad makes everything sound so simple. Why do adults make everything so complicated? Because we have to think about everything, instead of doing what's in our hearts. Teri needs me. I know she needs me, but she won't admit it. I'm supposed to be her friend, one of her best friends, and she can't even tell me she needs me.*

Damon shook his head and sighed. *What kind of foundation is that to build a relationship on?*

* * *

Teri sat in bed, trying to finish another book. She had purchased several other books on relationships, and she was starting to see herself in several places. "Damn." She took off her glasses and leaned back in the pillows to relax her back. "I really do have some issues."

Fear of intimacy, fear of rejection, fear, fear, fear. I have got to face this thing once and for all.

She found her purse and took out her cell phone and scrolled down to Damon's name. She sat there for almost half an hour trying to talk herself into pressing the talk button, so the call would go through.

"I can't do it. It's no use." She cut off the light and pushed the book and her notepad aside. "Mama always said my pride would kill me." As she slid under the heavy comforter, her cell phone fell out of the bed and onto the floor. "Maybe tomorrow," she whispered as she fell asleep.

Damon's ears were ringing when he left the club. He usually enjoyed listening to his favorite jams through a high-tech audio system, but tonight the music seemed overly loud and it irritated him.

His brother, A.C., had met him in California. He was assisting Damon with the first concert in Los Angeles. Damon had another meeting in the Bay Area on Monday morning, so A.C., gregarious by nature, had crammed their short weekend with back-to-back activities. Once the business had been handled, wine, women, and song were the theme of every night.

"I must be getting old." Damon laughed. "I can't believe you had me out in a club until . . ." He paused to look at his watch. "Two-thirty? No wonder I'm tired."

"Tired and old." His brother laughed.

Damon smiled and gave his brother a hug when they arrived back at the home in Hollywood Hills where they were staying. It belonged to an old girl-friend of his brother's, who worked as a model and a flight attendant. He would be leaving in the morning. He climbed the stairs to the bedroom designated as his while he was in town. *I wonder what's really going on with Teri.*

It was quiet in the hills . . . so quiet, it was loud and disturbing. He thought he heard crickets as he undressed for bed. He was thinking about his bed in Teri's house when he realized there was a constant beeping mingled with the crickets' chirps.

He sat up in the bed. *Now what the hell is that?* He looked around the room and realized his cell phone was beeping. He checked his voice mail, but there was no message, so he scrolled through the phone to see whose number was in the caller ID. He was shocked when he saw Teri's cell phone number displayed. *She actually called me, but she didn't leave a message.*

He cut on the light and sat thinking about the conversation he had earlier with Ahmad. It was too late to call her now, and since she hadn't left a message he wasn't sure what to think. *Is she actually reaching out for me?*

Damon found that hard to believe, but her number was right there in his phone. A smile eased onto his handsome face.

twenty-three

teri sat on the floor in J&H, stacking cans of vegetables and fruit on the shelves and listening to the rain pelt the building and the streets. She had spent most of the day unpacking and shelving canned goods. It was somewhat tedious, but she had enjoyed coordinating the various cans by size, shape, and color.

It had been an extraordinarily quiet day. The store phone or her cell phone hadn't rung once. Teri got up and walked into the office to pick up the phone to make sure the rain hadn't knocked out a phone line, but the monotonous dial tone assured her that was not the case.

She looked at the desk for some clue to Maxine's whereabouts. She hadn't heard from her or Bird the entire day. It was strange, not talking to her sisters. When would this disagreement end? It was normal for the them to quarrel, but never over anything as major as this.

She sat down behind the desk and immediately thought of the day she found that newspaper on Damon's desk. *I need my own desk, my own office, and a life to go with it. I am getting out of here.*

She was tossing her things back inside her briefcase when the telephone rang. Its loudness startled her after being alone all day in the store. Answering it, Teri was surprised to hear her nephew's voice. He called the store daily to let his mom know when he was home from school, but it was long past that time now.

"Ahmad, is everything okay?"

"Yes. Are you okay, Aunt Teri?"

"I'm fine, Ahmad. Do you need a ride home or something?"

"I got home a while ago. Mom picked me up. I just wanted to know if you'd pick me up after basketball practice tomorrow?"

"Your mom can't do it?"

"She has a lot of things to do tomorrow, so I was hoping you would be able to. Maybe I could come by afterward for dinner and we could play chess?"

"You think you're going to beat me?"

Tears welled up in her eyes and spilled down her cheeks. She loved Ahmad as though he was her own son, and to see him would do wonders for her aching heart.

"Sure, Ahmad, I'll be there."

She finished packing up and tried to think of

something to do in order to avoid going home and thinking of Damon. She found a newspaper and quickly scanned the movie section, then tossed it aside. *I don't want to go alone.*

She considered her alternatives. Normally, her schedule was so tight she rarely had free time. Being away from law was forcing her to confront a lot of issues she had never dealt with, due to sheer lack of time. Like the way having Damon around had really filled a void she hadn't noticed, until he left. *People take each other for granted entirely too much.* She tried not to think about her sisters. Her family occupied a lot of her time, too. *No Maxine, Bird, and Damon, or a job.* "I have no life," she whispered.

Finally, Teri decided to stop by the bookstore for a fresh supply of books. She had forced herself to finish the book on relationships, so at least she'd be more informed for her next relationship.

Damon finished up his last meeting and headed toward the airport. For some reason, everyone wanted to fly to Chicago that day and all of the flights were booked. He was going standby on the first thing available, preferably the midnight flight that would get him back to Chicago in the morning. He returned his rental car and hung out by the gate where his flight would depart, eating some Chinese food he picked up in the terminal. *I still can't believe she called.*

*   *   *

Teri tried not to focus on her disappointment when she discovered there were no messages on her home phone. She scanned through the caller ID to see if anyone had called and hung up, but no luck there, either. She poured a glass of wine to have with the teriyaki chicken and rice she had picked up. While she ate, she tried to read a book, but it didn't hold her attention. She was just plain, old miserable.

Damon arrived in Chicago around noon. He had gotten a seat on a very early flight after camping out all night in the airport. He had never spent the night in an airport, but there was a first time for everything. He stopped by his father's house to retrieve his car, and drove to Teri's to shower and change. He tried to take a nap, but he wasn't sleepy.

Teri placed her last can on the shelf for the day. She had endured another day of solitude and canned goods. She had spoken briefly with Maxine, who was busy running around the city, trying to find another place to hold the dinner. She couldn't help the twinge of jealousy she felt for her sister's busyness.

It was still raining when Teri made the drive to Ahmad's school. She smiled, looking forward to spending time with her nephew. After parking, she went into the gymnasium and took a seat on the bleachers with the parents watching the practice.

She caught Ahmad's attention as he ran up the

court for the next layup, and waved. *You're never going to have your own children.* It was that nagging voice in her head again. *Your biological clock is ticking. You don't have a husband. You don't even have a boyfriend.*

I'm going to have all of that, she answered in her mind.

The conversation wasn't new. With each birthday, she constantly battled the fact that she was getting older and no closer to having a lasting, loving relationship that would eventually produce children. She felt herself getting anxious, and her breathing became a little uneven. *Oh no, not here. Not now.*

She decided to go outside for some air and stood up. She felt a little wobbly, when a strong hand suddenly steadied her.

"I thought I might find you here."

She knew it was him without even looking . . . his smell, his touch, his voice, the electricity that shot through her body from head to toe the moment he touched her.

"What are you doing here, Damon?" She slowly looked up into his eyes.

"I came by to see my boy practice." He smiled.

"I thought you were in California."

"I just got back today."

"And you had nothing better to do than to come to my nephew's basketball practice?"

Teri felt herself growing more upset by the minute, probably because he hadn't bothered to phone her once.

"Do you have a problem with me being here, Teri? Just say so, and I'll leave."

"Yes, I do have a problem with you being here, but obviously Ahmad invited you, so stay."

Damon frownned. "Teri, what's going on? You act like you never called me."

"I called you?" she asked huffily.

"Yes, you did, and now you want to lie about it."

"I did not call you, Damon."

"You're calling me a liar?"

Teri stiffened. "Yes, if you want to keep insisting that I called you."

"I went through a lot of trouble to get back here, because I thought you needed me. And this is the thanks I get . . . your self-righteous attitude? I've had enough of this crap." He turned to leave.

Teri's breathing became uneven. "I don't know what you're talking about. I didn't call you, I don't need you, and I never asked you to come back."

"You don't get it, Teri. You just don't get it." He looked her up and down with an expression she had never seen on his face. "It's becoming more than obvious that you are incapable of dealing with your feelings. Now I understand why you're alone."

"I don't have to stand here and listen to this." He pushed the same button Lem and Kenny had pressed, along with everyone else she had trusted with her feelings. She turned to walk away, but Damon caught her by the hand.

"You're not leaving; you have to take Ahmad home."

"No, you can take him home, since you insist on hanging around my family. I have to go." Her breathing was becoming worse, and she had to breathe through her mouth.

"Hey, Aunt Teri. Hi, Damon." Ahmad ran up and gave them both a hug.

"Hi, sweetie." Teri was shaking as she fumbled in her bag for a bottle of water.

"Aunt Teri, are you okay?" Ahmad's young face clouded over with concern.

"Yes, Ahmad. I'm fine. But I have to go." She kissed him on the cheek and headed toward the exit.

As she walked away Damon thought he saw her stumble, but she pushed open the gymnasium door and left the building.

"Ahmad, what's up?" Damon tried to feign his best smile.

"You and Aunt Teri were fighting, weren't you?"

Damon let out a long sigh. "That's not how I intended for things to go."

"She didn't look so good. Let's go." Ahmad trotted toward the exit and Damon followed.

"What do you mean she didn't look so good?"

Damon pushed open the doors and they were in the parking lot.

Teri's hands were shaking as she fumbled for her keys and opened the car door. "Oh, my God," she whispered. "Please don't let this happen; not here, not now."

She managed to find the pills and took two. She sat in the car, attempting to regulate her breathing and drinking water. *When is that medicine going to work?*

Damon and Ahmad searched the parking lot for her car.

"There she is." Ahmad pointed out the car and they ran toward it.

Teri looked up and saw them coming toward her. "Oh, no. I can't let them see me like this."

She tried to start the car, but she couldn't breathe. When they reached the car, she was gasping for breath. She tried to say *help,* but the words weren't there. Tears streamed out of her eyes as she fought with all her power to take a breath.

"Aunt Teri! Aunt Teri!"

Damon pulled out his cell phone and called for an ambulance. Tears came to his eyes as he watched her struggling to breathe. He sat next to her in the passenger's seat and rolled down the window. The chilly early evening air seemed to help. He looked into her eyes, filled with fear. Moments later her breathing began to smooth out, and he held her in his arms as she cried.

Ahmad was still upset.

"Pull yourself together, little man. We've got to be strong for her. You wouldn't want her to see you upset like this."

Ahmad sniffed and agreed. Damon was just as frightened as Ahmad.

"I'm okay now, Ahmad. Don't worry." Teri was barely able to speak above a whisper.

The sound of sirens was growing louder.

"I hear the ambulance, Damon."

"Me, too."

A few spectators had gathered in the parking lot. They stood around watching to see what would happen next as the paramedics pulled into the lot, jumped out, ran over to the car, and began talking to Damon. Moments later, they rolled a gurney over to the car and lifted Teri out onto it.

"What's going on? Where are you taking me?" She tried to sit up.

"Just lie down and relax, Teri," the paramedic instructed.

"Just be cool, baby. You need to go to the hospital and let them check you out. You scared the crap out of me back there." Damon held her hand as the gurney was moved toward the ambulance.

"Hospital? I don't need to go to the hospital; I'm fine." She was still **try**ing to get up when they hoisted the cot up into the truck.

"We'll be right behind you," he told her.

As the paramedics began checking her vital signs and hooked her up to some oxygen, Teri continually informed them, "I'm fine." But the oxygen did seem to help the fog in her head.

Ahmad was on the cell phone calling Maxine while Damon followed the flashing lights of the ambulance.

It's all my fault. I should have never come here. I should have just stayed in California.

twenty-four

When they wheeled Teri into the emergency room, she had never felt so embarrassed in her life.

She saw Damon carrying her purse and Ahmad close behind, and wondered why he had returned from California so suddenly and why he had insisted that she had phoned him.

They took her into an examining room. A nurse brought in a gown and Teri quickly undressed and climbed on the table under a sheet.

Damon stuck his head inside the room. "Is it okay if I come inside?" She nodded and he took a seat beside her. "Ahmad called Maxine, so I know your sisters are on the way."

"That really wasn't necessary." She spoke softly.

"You know you couldn't keep Bird and Maxine away even if you wanted to. Is there anything I can get you?"

"No."

He sat there looking at her curled up in a fetal position under the sheet.

"I'm sorry."

"Sorry for what?" Her eyes seemed huge and she looked very frail, not at all like the woman he had argued with less than an hour ago.

"I'm sorry for whatever I did that got you in here." There were tears in his eyes, and she immediately wanted to comfort him.

"This isn't your fault," she whispered. "It's mine. I should have been taking my medication."

Maxine burst in the room and interrupted their conversation. "Teri, what happened? Are you okay? What happened, Damon?" She looked at him, and then Teri.

"I'm going to sit with Ahmad, so you two can talk." He quickly wiped away a tear from his eye. He handed Maxine her sister's purse and left. Maxine waited until he was out of the room.

"Teri, what happened?" She sat down and smoothed her sister's hair.

"I'm fine, Maxine." Teri managed a smile.

"You are not fine. If you were fine, we wouldn't be sitting in the ER."

"I had a panic attack and Damon brought me here." Teri shifted on the small, uncomfortable table. She really just wanted to go home and get in her own comfortable bed.

Outside, Bird and Lem rushed into the waiting room with Jay.

"Where's Teri?" Bird was on the verge of tears. "Is she okay?"

"Maxine's with her in the examining room." Damon found his voice somewhere.

"Lem, you and Jay stay out here with them," Bird commanded.

Lem sat down with Damon and Ahmad, while Bird raced to the examining room.

"Teri? Teri? Teri, where are you?" They could hear Bird coming long before they saw her.

"Let me go get this child before she wakes the living dead." Maxine poked her head out and beckoned her sister.

"Teri, what happened?" Bird burst into tears without hearing her answer.

"I had a panic attack."

"Why? Where? I thought you weren't having them anymore." Bird couldn't wait to hear anything, she just cried.

"Bird." Teri attempted to sit up and comfort her little sister.

"Good evening, ladies." A handsome African American doctor walked into the room. He smiled and it was like the sunshine after the rain. "I'm Dr. Anthony Michaels. Now, which one of you ladies is Teri Joseph?"

"She is," Bird and Maxine chorused.

Teri remained silent. *Why didn't I just take that damn medication? I hate it that Damon had to see me this way.*

"Ms. Joseph, what seems to be the problem?" He looked her directly in the eyes.

"I had a panic attack."

"Are you in any pain?" He carefully examined her head and looked into her eyes.

"I have a headache."

They watched him examine her and scribble notes on a chart.

"Are you on any medication?"

"Just these." She motioned for Maxine to give her the purse, and produced the bottle of pills Dr. Pruit had prescribed.

He took the bottle and continued scribbling notes. "I'm going to order an MRI and a series of other X rays. We'll draw some blood, give you something for your headache, and then evaluate the situation once I have all the results from the lab and radiology.

"Okay," Bird and Maxine answered for her.

He laughed. "Is that okay with you, Teri?"

"Whatever you have to do. I just want to go home."

"That's what we all want: for you to go home. I'll be back shortly." He left the room as swiftly as he had entered.

Teri was relieved when the nurse gave her a shot. It soothed every ounce of pain and every raw nerve in her body. She was asleep when they carted her off to radiology.

In the waiting room, Damon passed around cheeseburgers and fries to everyone. He had no appetite. The only thing he could think of was Teri, and of his being the cause of them all being there. *I'll never forgive myself for this.* He was about to go outside when Bird came out.

"What happened, Damon?" She was calmer than she had been earlier.

"We were talking . . . no, we were arguing." He couldn't hold back the tears. "It's all my fault."

"What's all your fault?"

Damon sighed deeply. "We were in the gym and she was upset because I was there. Ahmad called me in California. Something about the house and how no one was there for her. Then she called me."

"She did?"

"Yes, but she didn't leave a message. Ahmad was concerned about her, so he and I planned it so she and I would both be there to meet him after school, so we'd have to talk."

"Maxine said Teri told her you were moving out of the house."

"I was thinking about it. I even made some calls, but I never told her. We were having some problems so I thought it would be better if I moved out. She came up to my office and found the newspaper with the ads I'd circled."

"Damn. Y'all got issues." Bird rummaged in a bag, found a cheeseburger, and grabbed a few fries.

"Tell me about it." He flopped down in a chair away from the others. "I'm no good for her."

"Don't even go there. You're the best thing that ever happened to her, and she's scared to death."

"Yeah. So scared, she had one of those attacks trying to get away from me."

"I wouldn't say that. There's a lot you don't know about."

"What happened?"

"You could say we all kind of ganged up on her with the house. Lem and I are moving out and Maxine and Kenny are selling their house and moving in, except Teri won't sell her share to Maxine, so we all got into a huge fight."

"You guys had a fight with her, too?" He rubbed his head trying to relieve some of the stress that was consuming every fiber of his being. "So, that's what Ahmad was talking about. I came home to be here for her, but she jumped all over me."

"That's my sister. Mama always warned her about being so prideful."

"But she did call me, Bird, and she kept insisting she didn't."

"Maybe her cell phone dialed yours by mistake. That used to happen to me all the time."

"You're kidding?"

"It happens more often than you'd think. People

have told me they can hear me talking. The talk button pushes against something, and it calls the number." Bird ate a few more fries.

"That explanation never crossed my mind. I just ran home to rescue her."

"Bird." Maxine had come into the waiting room. "The doctor wants to talk to us."

Bird popped the last of the burger in her mouth. "Don't you go anywhere, Damon."

The doctor was waiting for them in Teri's room.

"I understand you ladies are Ms. Joseph's sisters?"

"Yes," Maxine said.

"What kind of work does she do?" He took out a pen to take more notes.

"Teri's an attorney, but she hasn't been practicing law. We've been working on the reopening of our family's grocery store for Thanksgiving."

"You mean the big dinner they've been advertising on the radio with the Morning Team?"

"Yes." Maxine smiled.

"You listen to the radio?" Bird was clearly shocked.

"Of course I do." Dr. Michaels laughed. "I love hip-hop and R&B."

"You *do?*" Bird was still in shock.

"You'll have to come to our dinner, if we still have it," Maxine offered.

"You're not thinking about cancelling, are you? It's such a wonderful event."

"We're not planning to cancel, but we're still looking for a site," Maxine said.

"Oh, please don't cancel. I still can't believe that I've been fortunate to meet the ladies responsible for this spectacular event."

The door opened and Teri was wheeled back in the room. She got back up on the gurney under her sheet. It had become her security blanket, shielding her from the world.

"Can I go home now?" Teri demanded as soon as she saw the doctor.

"How are you feeling, sweetie?" Maxine was ever the nurturing mother, even when it came to her sisters.

"I feel fine," Teri said impatiently. "I just want to go home."

"I'd like to keep you overnight for observation," Dr. Michaels said. "Twenty-four hours from now, if everything checks out okay, I'll spring you from this joint." He smiled.

"Whatever you say, Dr. Michaels." Maxine smiled.

"I'll make all the arrangements." He left the room and the sisters looked at one another.

"This really isn't necessary. I'm going home." Teri threw back the sheet, and Maxine and Bird rushed to stop her.

"What do you think you're doing?" Bird folded her arms and stuck out a hip.

"You better get back in that bed." Maxine pulled the sheet back up. "What is your problem?"

Teri stared up at all the equipment attached to the ceiling. "I guess I do have a problem. I thought I was over those stupid panic attacks."

"You're still holding things in, Teri. Until you learn how to deal with things when they bother you, you might always have them." Maxine kissed her on the cheek.

"You need anything, Teri?" Bird was standing over her, too.

"Yes, could you ask the nurse if I can have another shot? Since the two of you are such a pain in the behind," she added with a hint of a smile.

Maxine went for the nurse and Bird sat down beside her.

"Damon's out there, blaming himself for everything. You should talk to him. He came back because he thought you called him."

"He kept saying that, but I never called him."

"But I bet your phone did. Mine used to do it a lot. It would dial the last person that phoned me, or randomly land on names in my phone book."

"Really?"

"Yes, until I locked the keypad."

"I was thinking about calling Damon," Teri confessed. "I scrolled down to his name, but I never pressed the send button."

"Well, something did. I'm just glad your phone called him, or else he wouldn't be here."

"Probably not," Teri said quietly.

"I tried to tell him, but it needs to come from you," Bird told her sternly.

"I'll talk to him."

"When?"

The nurse came in and administered the shot and Teri floated away into a world where there were no problems to contend with.

"She's asleep." She heard Maxine whisper.

Dr. Michaels returned and informed them that she was about to be moved to a room.

"There's nothing left for you ladies to do this evening, so why don't you go on home? Your sister's tests are fine; she really just needs to rest. If there's any change, we'll notify you."

Teri heard the entire conversation. *Good. Maybe now I can have some peace.*

"Okay," her sisters agreed reluctantly. They kissed her and left the room.

Teri was still awake when she was moved to a private room. She was about to get up when she heard footsteps, so she continued to pretend she was asleep.

"I'm sorry, Teri," she heard Damon whisper. "I never meant to hurt you. I love you." He kissed her gently on the lips, then he was gone.

She was no longer able to hold back the tears. She cried until there were no more tears left to cry. "I don't have to keep having these stupid attacks," she whispered. "I just need to admit that I need Damon."

twenty-five

teri was awake, watching the morning news shows, when Dr. Michaels came in her room.

"May I go home now? Please?" she immediately asked.

"You have my permission to depart the premises after lunch. And with that, I'm releasing you a little early." He sat down in the chair beside her bed. "I understand you're an attorney. I expect law can be a little stressful."

"It can be," she agreed. "But I'm not practicing right now."

"Good. Because I'm releasing you with only one instruction."

"What's that?" Teri smoothed her bathrobe.

"That you are to go home and do absolutely nothing."

"What?" Teri sat up straight in bed. It was the nothingness in her life that had rewarded her with an overnight visit to the hospital.

"I understand that's very hard for you to do. But there are some things you haven't wanted to face, and like most of the human race, instead of facing those things, you've covered them up with more activities."

"And you know this because . . . ?"

"I had a long talk with your sisters and your family. All of them are very nice people who love you very much."

"I can't believe they told a complete stranger my business."

"I understand completely." He smiled.

Teri folded her arms. "It seems like you already know everything, so I'll just let you keep talking."

"They're all very concerned about you, Ms. Joseph. They've told me all about your panic attacks, the disagreement you all had over your mother's property, and Damon."

Damn, did they tell you what size underwear I wear?

"So, I'm releasing you on that one condition. Take it easy and do nothing. I had a conversation with Dr. Pruit, also. He wants to see you in a week."

Teri watched him scribble more notes in a file.

"Otherwise you may find yourself back in here, and next time you may not be so lucky."

He handed Teri the release forms for her to sign. She eyed him carefully before she took the pen and signed the papers. She didn't like him knowing all her personal business.

"I heard your sister on the radio talking about all the things going on for Thanksgiving. I couldn't help wondering what kind of family would put such effort and care into the community on a family holiday, and then suddenly all of you were sitting in my examining room. Seems like kismet, if you ask me."

He looked at Teri, who offered no response.

"Don't be too hard on them. They really do love you. All of them." He took the release form and was gone.

Teri picked at the breakfast that was brought in and spent the rest of her morning watching television, a luxury she was never afforded, because she was always too busy. Now that all of her personal drama had been exposed, she felt so relaxed.

She lay back on the pillows and wondered what she had been so afraid of.

Loving Damon and him not loving me back. He told me he loved me last night. A smile lit up her face. *But I'm sure he said it out of guilt.*

"Don't do this to yourself, Teri." *That's what was making me so crazy before.* "I'm just going to wait and see what happens, and whatever it is, I'll deal with it."

"What are you smiling about?" Maxine walked in with a change of clothes.

"I'm just happy to see my sister here, so we can blow this joint."

"So, you're going to stick to the doctor's orders?" Maxine asked on the drive home.

"Yes, Maxine." Teri laid her head on her sister's shoulder.

"Teri." There was a funny sound in Maxine's voice. "Please don't keep things in anymore. None of us would be able to make it, if you weren't here to boss us around." Her voice was choked with tears.

Teri began crying, too. "I'm getting better. I promise."

"I know you are."

They both sniffed as Teri found tissues in her bag. She handed one to her sister.

"Stop crying." Maxine dabbed at her eyes.

"I will if you will." Teri blew her nose, and they both finally laughed.

"You silly . . ." Maxine was at a red light. She leaned over and kissed Teri on the cheek. "I love you."

"I love you, too."

"Think you can say it to Damon, now?"

"He said it last night. But he thought I was asleep."

"Why didn't you let him know you weren't?"

"I don't know. Probably because I was surprised, overjoyed . . ."

"Brain dead." Maxine was laughing.

"Yeah, that, too." Teri smiled at Maxine and kissed her again. "I'm hungry. Will you make me some real breakfast when we get to the house?"

"Sure, what would you like?"

"Scrambled eggs, a little bacon."

"Grits with cheese." They laughed together.

"Anything else?"

"Have some with me?"

"But of course." Maxine smiled at Teri.

"What would I ever do without you?"

"Starve."

They were both laughing as they got out of the car and went into Teri's house.

"While we're on the subject of food . . . it looks like we're going to have to cancel the dinner. I couldn't find anyplace to have it."

"We're not cancelling our wonderful Thanksgiving dinner."

"We're not?"

"No. I made a few phone calls while I was waiting on you to pick me up, and it's all worked out."

"But you promised you wouldn't do anything," Maxine protested.

"I just made a few phone calls. So sue me." Teri smiled triumphantly.

"So, where are we having it?"

"At the store."

"But you said there wasn't enough room." Maxine looked puzzled.

"Maxine, do you remember when we were little and Daddy would barbecue, and we would feed the entire neighborhood?" Teri sat on the sofa and Maxine joined her.

"I'll never forget it. We used to have so much fun."

"Well, the Josephs are feeding the neighborhood once again on Thanksgiving."

"But how?"

"It's all been taken care of." Teri seemed to glow from within. "Daddy would be so proud."

twenty-six

maxine made breakfast, placed everything on a tray, and brought it into the living room. She had added home fries, toast, and hot chocolate to her sister's menu. Teri devoured everything in a matter of minutes.

"You *were* hungry. I've got a pan of lasagna in the fridge for you, too, and a schedule." Maxine took Teri by the arm and they walked upstairs to her bedroom together.

"A schedule? What kind of schedule?"

"We didn't know what was up with you and Damon, so we made a schedule for your meals and who's going to be at the house with you."

"No," Teri interrupted. "I can be alone. You guys have things to do."

"You don't have an opinion," Maxine reminded her. "And because you're so hardheaded, someone will be with you around the clock."

Maxine pulled the comforter back on Teri's bed and fluffed the pillows.

"You even changed my linen? When did you guys have time to do all of this?" Teri looked around her bedroom. "Someone cleaned the house, too. I wondered when we were downstairs, but now I know it for a fact." The carpet had been freshly vacuumed and her books were all neatly stacked beside the bed. "Did you clean my house, Maxine?"

"No, I can't take credit for that. Damon did."

"Damon? Is he still here?" While they were eating, she had looked around for some sort of indication that he hadn't moved out.

"He stayed here last night."

Teri jumped off the bed and tore into his bedroom. When she saw that his suitcase and garment bag were lying on the bed, she sighed with relief.

"You guys need to talk." Maxine walked her back into her bedroom, and ran some bathwater.

"Don't leave, Maxine. Stay with me while I take my bath so we can talk."

"Who said I was leaving?"

Teri smiled warmly at her sister from a sea of bubbles. She had always spent so much time alone, studying, working. . . . She had gotten used to it, especially since Maxine and Bird were married with families of their own, but now she craved companionship.

"I was afraid Damon had moved out," she said

softly. "When we walked in the house, I looked around but I couldn't tell." Tears gathered in her eyes, but she continued. "There was no indication of him being here, because I never allowed him to put his things in the house. Everything says Teri. Nothing said Damon. I really am selfish . . . and controlling. How does he put up with me?"

"Because he loves you." Maxine handed her a tissue to wipe away the tears that were healing her aching heart and soul, then left the bathroom and returned with a telephone. "Why don't you call him?"

Teri nodded and dialed his cell phone. She had to smile when she felt herself tingle, the way she always did whenever she heard his voice.

"Are you moving out, Damon?" She cut straight to the chase.

"Do you want me to move out?"

"Not if you don't want to. I want you to stay," she said.

"Good, because I'd like to stay. Can I bring you anything?"

"No, but thank you. Maxine made lasagna for dinner. I'll see you when you get here."

Teri was smiling when she hung up the phone.

"That wasn't so hard." Maxine walked back into the bathroom and handed her a towel. "Look at you, you're glowing."

"Damon's not moving out. He's going to stay."

"I'm happy for you."

"Maxine, about the house . . ."

"We're not talking about that now, Teri."

"Yes, we are. I haven't made a decision, but I'll make one soon."

"It's not important, Teri."

"Yes, it is. And I don't want you thinking that had anything to do with me having a panic attack. I just had a lot going on, and I was trying to work through it by myself."

"Like you always do. I hope you and Damon work things out. He really loves you, Teri," Maxine said.

"I'm finally beginning to realize that." The tears slid out of her eyes and down her cheeks yet again.

"Oh, Teri." Maxine pulled her sister into her arms. "Don't you think you deserve to be loved?" Maxine smoothed her hair while she spoke.

"Yes," Teri managed. "I deserve to be loved."

twenty-seven

bird arrived at Teri's house just after Damon. She pulled up behind him and watched him get out of the car with a long floral box and an enormous teddy bear.

"Look at you." She grinned.

"Nothing but the best for my girl." He smiled.

"That's what I'm talking about." Bird grabbed the bear as they went into the house.

Maxine was on the phone in the living room, with papers all around her. She ended her conversation and joined Bird and Damon in the kitchen.

"Are those roses, Damon?" Maxine found a crystal vase in the dining room.

"Why don't you give them to her in the box?" Bird suggested.

"Stay out of it, Bird, and let him do it his way."

Damon tiptoed up the stairs with the box of roses and the teddy bear. Maxine and Bird were out of sight, but within listening distance. Teri was reading a book when he came into the room.

"Hey, you." He handed her the box and the bear.

"Damon, what is all of this? I'm not sick."

Bird made a face. "Has she got a romantic bone left in her body?"

"Be quiet, so we can hear," Maxine whispered back.

Teri slowly untied the bow on the box of flowers and gasped when she saw more than a dozen long-stem red roses.

"Damon. These are gorgeous!"

He was sitting on the bed beside her, and she reached for his face and kissed him gently on the lips.

"She'd *better* be smacking those lips," Bird whispered.

"You are so bad." Maxine covered her mouth to keep from laughing.

Damon smiled as he watched her open the accompanying card that read, *Faithfully.* She looked at him for an explanation.

"You're my best friend and you've always been there for me, and now I intend to be here for you, as long as you allow me."

Maxine grabbed Bird.

"You once asked me why I didn't love you enough to be faithful."

"I remember," Teri said softly.

"I can't answer that question. I've asked myself

hundreds of times and I couldn't come up with an answer, except that it was the stupidest thing I've ever done, and . . ."

Maxine and Bird grabbed each other.

"I love you, Teri Joseph. Despite everything, I've never stopped loving you, and that's why I'm giving you this bear named Faithful—as a reminder to you that I have loved you, do love you, and will always love you—faithfully."

Maxine covered Bird's mouth to keep her from squealing.

Teri was speechless. She took the bear, stroked it gently, then hugged it and cried.

"Have I finally found the man who loves me for who I am and the way I am, and not for the things I do, hoping to win his love?"

"Yes, Teri Joseph, you have."

Damon held her in his arms and cried with her, while Bird and Maxine gathered up their things and quietly left the house.

twenty-eight

teri listened to the rain that continued to drench the city, with Thanksgiving only a day away. She rolled over and watched Damon sleeping. He looked so peaceful, she hated to wake him. She only wished the two of them could lie in her bed forever, because together they'd found a small piece of heaven on earth.

Maxine was also listening to the rain as she scrambled eggs for breakfast. Everything was ready for the Thanksgiving Day dinner, except the weather. "Rain, rain, go away. Come again some other day."

"Are you going to Aunt Teri's today?" Ahmad asked as he entered the kitchen.

"Yes. And I'll be taking the girls with me, so you'll be able to study for that big chemistry exam. You're always complaining about how you need peace and quiet. You'll have plenty of it today."

"Can't I study over there?"

Maxine smiled understandingly. "You want to see Teri, don't you?"

"Yeah." He smiled.

Bird looked at all the packing boxes in the living and dining rooms of the house. There were more packing boxes in the kitchen, where Lem was feeding Jay. It seemed like boxes were everywhere.

"It's a good thing we're going to have Thanksgiving at the store. This place is a mess," she said.

Yeah, it is a mess." Lem looked around the kitchen, too.

Bird stepped over a box to get to the refrigerator. They had been turned down for several more loans, but the condo hadn't been sold yet and it was still on the market. She looked at her husband and contemplated telling him she was going to apply for the loan in her name, but she knew how much it would hurt him. She bit her lip and sighed as she closed the refrigerator. *If I did that, it would crush Lem, and I love my man too much to do that.*

Teri's words still stung Lem, but however harsh, they were true. He wasn't able to get his wife and son a place to live. He thought about the boxes he had begun to pack. Bird had finally started packing, too. He was determined that the Van Adamses were moving, somewhere, somehow.

* * *

Damon opened his eyes and smiled when he saw Teri was awake. He could hear the rain gently pelting the roof and he snuggled closer to her, enjoying feeling her body next to his and the smell of her favorite shower gel.

"Why didn't you wake me?" He closed the book she was reading and pulled her into his arms.

"Because you looked so peaceful." She smiled as she gently stroked his face.

He kissed her, then rolled out of bed.

"What would you like for breakfast this morning?"

"You."

"My kind of breakfast." He laughed. "But I'm going to make you some sausage and French toast, so Maxine won't fire me from my job."

"She can't fire you, because I do all the hiring around here . . . besides, I'm fine. I don't know why you guys are making such a big deal. There's too many things going on right now for everyone to wait on me hand and foot."

"*You* are a big deal."

She tugged on his hand, indicating that she wanted him to get back into bed.

"Teri . . . I'm going to run you some bathwater."

"But if I have to stay in bed, I give you permission to stay in here with me," she flirted.

"Teri . . ."

The doorbell rang before she could say another word.

"Reinforcements." He laughed and went to answer the door while Teri got up to take a bath.

When Bird and Maxine walked into Teri's living room, Damon greeted them with a kiss and ran upstairs with a warm towel fresh out of the dryer for Teri.

"Things are certainly looking pretty cozy around here." Bird smiled at Maxine.

Kenny sat at his desk, holding his head in his hands.

"It's not your fault, man."

"Well, whose fault is it?" Kenny looked at Lem, waiting for an answer.

"Damon was trying to blame himself. Bird and Maxine, too. Me, you . . . we're all blaming ourselves, but it's nobody's fault."

"Oh, yeah? Then why did it happen? What's the point?" Kenny was angry and he didn't know why.

"I think it's a lesson, man. For all of us, including Teri."

Kenny didn't look convinced.

"We walk through life and we take a lot of things for granted. Every once in a while, something happens that makes us realize life is short. It's a gift, and we shouldn't take it or the people we love for granted."

Just then dispatch paged Lem for a job, so their conversation ended.

Kenny watched him drive away. "The young brother makes a lot of sense."

"Think they did it yet?" Bird whispered as they climbed the stairs.

"Bird." Maxine blushed for her sister.

"All I know is, something better be going on up in here, after what we heard the other day."

"You're terrible."

Teri was sitting in bed reading when they walked in.

"She's wearing her Victoria's Secret nightgown," Bird whispered.

"What are you guys up to now?" Teri smiled.

"She got some!" Bird whispered excitedly.

"No, I didn't, Bird." Teri nearly fell out of her bed laughing. "You think you know everything, but you couldn't be more wrong."

"And you're happy about this because . . ." Bird looked at Teri like she was crazy.

"Because you think you're so accurate when it comes to predicting my love life." Teri was still laughing and Maxine joined in. "But when Damon and I do make love . . . you'll be the first to know." Teri grinned.

"Right. Moving right along . . . Teri, what is going on at the store?"

"The street's been blocked off, and they're setting up a tent in the street in front of the store," Maxine reported.

"Really?" Teri feigned concern. "Didn't you say the radio station was coming, Maxine?"

"She's not going to tell us anything, Bird."

"So, did you get a loan for the condo yet?" Teri focused on her youngest sister.

"Uh, yeah." Bird lied.

The doctor had advised them to keep Teri stress free.

"Congratulations. I'm so happy for you guys."

Bird managed a smile and looked at Maxine.

"Maxine, don't you think for one moment I'm not coming to the opening, and I'm also doing the radio interview at the station with the two of you. That is why you guys came over here, right? To take me to the radio station?"

"Yes." Maxine was in her closet. "Shall I assist the diva with her wardrobe selection, or will Damon be handling that?"

"I'll be taking care of that." Teri smiled at her sisters. "Now, is there anything else you'd like to discuss, ladies?"

twenty-nine

teri, Maxine, and Bird sat on stools wearing head-phones in the broadcast booth at the radio station with J.B. and Justine. They were all smiling and laughing as they sang along to Sister Sledge's classic "We Are Family."

It was hard for them all to keep still as they all sang, "I got all my sisters with me" into the microphones.

"No, ladies and gentlemen, it's not Sister Sledge, Destiny's Child, or 3LW. These three beautiful ladies are Chicago's own . . ." J.B. pointed at the girls.

"The Joseph sisters," they chorused.

"J&H Groceries was one of the businesses that was torched during the riots that nearly destroyed our close-knit community, but the Joseph family found the strength to fight their way back into business, and are feeding the needy in the community to celebrate."

Everyone was smiling as Justine gave listeners a brief history of the fall and rise of J&H Groceries.

"Now that we've heard all of these wonderful things going on at J&H, tell us more about you, the Joseph sisters, the force behind this commendable event." Justine looked at them and the girls looked at one another.

"We're sisters." Teri spoke into the mike. "We come from a very loving family with strong values and a deep love for the community."

"All right," J.B. cut in. "We want the real inside stuff. Who's the youngest?"

"I am," Bird piped up.

"So she got away with everything." Justine laughed.

"She sure did," Maxine replied as Teri laughed.

"Who's the bossiest?"

"Teri." Maxine and Bird laughed.

Kenny and Lem were grinning from ear to ear as they listened to the broadcast over the intercom at the garage. Everyone was gathered around the coffee table eating Krispy Kremes.

The deejays had a list of questions for the girls.

Damon listened from his car. He had gone to the bookstore for a fresh supply of reading material for Teri.

Everyone at Cut It Up was also listening to the broadcast.

* * *

J.B. repeated the information for the Thanksgiving Day dinner. "Any shout outs, ladies?"

"Yes." Bird spoke up first. "I'd just like to say happy turkey day to everyone, and a big one to my stylists at Cut It Up, where making you look beautiful is the name of the game, and I love you, Lem and Jay."

"You're right." J.B. laughed. "She does get away with everything. She just got away with the rest of your airtime."

"Bird!" Teri and Maxine chorused.

"I knew we'd see a fight in here sooner or later." J.B. laughed again.

"J.B. doesn't know how to behave himself with three beautiful sisters in the studios. Go ahead, ladies." Justine punched him in the arm. He was still laughing when Teri spoke.

"I'd just like to say we're looking forward to seeing everyone tomorrow at the grand reopening of J&H. And hello, Damon. Thanks for being a real friend."

"There she goes with that *friend* stuff," Bird whispered in Maxine's ear, breaking her concentration.

"Bird!" Maxine laughed into the microphone. "I just want to say hello to my husband, Kenny Chadway, and everyone at Chadway Towing, my son Ahmad, and my daughters, Kelly and Brooke. And thanks to the station and to you, J.B. and Justine, for all your wonderful support."

The broadcast continued as the ladies took off their headphones.

"We were actually on the radio!" Maxine screamed once they were out of the building.

"I know." Bird grinned. "That was so much fun."

"We are family," Teri sang as they walked to the car. She grabbed her sisters' arms and they danced around in a circle.

The three of them drove over to J&H. It was still sprinkling lightly, but workers were busy taking folding chairs and tables out of a truck.

"If it rains, everything will be ruined," Maxine worried.

"If? It *is* raining. We'll just have to make the best of it." Teri gasped when they walked into the store. Every shelf was stocked with every type of food, and the refrigerators and freezers were filled and running. "Look at this place!"

"J&H never looked this good," Maxine said.

"Never." Bird was amazed.

"I wanted it to be nice. Not everyone can afford to move to the suburbs, but that doesn't mean people don't want or shouldn't have somewhere nice to shop in their own community," Teri explained to her sisters.

She looked around at all the turkeys in the freezers, waiting to be distributed in gift baskets with all the fixings for needy families in the neighborhood.

"Maxine, this was such a wonderful idea . . . the dinner and the baskets."

Maxine beamed. "And that was really good thinking, Teri, making the last-minute calls to get this tent, the chairs and tables, and the heaters. Mama and Daddy would be so proud."

"You did it, Teri." Bird grinned. "When we walked in here for the first time that night, I never imagined all this."

"No, *we* did it." Teri hugged her sisters. "I would have never had the courage to do this without you."

thirty

To everyone's amazement, Thanksgiving Day was sunny and bright. The sky was clear and blue and the air was chilly and crisp. Teri issued the orders and everyone manned their posts. The radio station arrived and set up. There were several television news crews present, as well.

"God answered my prayer." Kenny smiled at Maxine.

"He sure did." She was radiantly happy.

"Congratulations, baby." They kissed as Ahmad walked by and smiled.

"I have a little something for you." Damon handed Teri a blue velvet jewelry box and smiled.

"Damon, what is this?" She looked at the box and then at him.

"A little something I picked up for you while I was in Los Angeles. I saw this and thought of you, so please don't deny me this pleasure." His eyes were twinkling and he looked like a mischievous little boy.

"All right." She opened the box and forgot to breathe when she saw the sparkling diamond tennis bracelet.

"Are you okay?" He was immediately concerned.

"I'm fine." She finally remembered to breathe. "I'm sorry, I didn't mean to frighten you. But . . . Damon!"

He took the bracelet out of the box and fastened it around her wrist. "Remember those friendship bracelets people used to give each other?"

"But Damon!"

"They say diamonds are forever, so just think of this as an everlasting friendship bracelet."

"I love you." She pulled his face toward her and kissed him gently on the lips.

"I love you, too."

"There you are. " Bird came in the office and pulled them apart. "Y'all are gonna have to take a time-out. Everyone's looking for you, Teri. Would you put on some lipstick, so we can get this party started?" She winked at Damon while Teri freshened her makeup, then dragged them both out of the office and into the store.

A gentleman from the mayor's office read a proclamation honoring the Josephs for their countless contributions to the community, and the cutting of the ribbon followed. All three sisters held on to the gigantic pair of scissors Bird had found and spray-painted gold. The store was overflowing with people and every type of food imaginable.

Teri read over the piece of paper she'd written upon, folded it, stuck it inside an envelope, and sealed it. She wrote Ahmad's name across it and went to look for her nephew.

There were plenty of volunteers to serve food, and Maxine had organized them into shifts. Kenny and Damon worked side by side while they handed out food baskets.

"Happy Thanksgiving, Damon." Kenny grinned.

"Happy Thanksgiving, Kenny Chadway."

"I wanted to spend some time with you to offer you some advice on how to handle a Joseph woman, but things have been really busy at the garage lately."

Teri walked by and waved, and Damon waved back.

"But it looks like you've got the situation under control." Kenny smiled again.

"Hey, Ahmad." Keisha walked up to the table where he was serving hot food. "This is really great. Thanks for inviting me." She looked around at all of the activity in and around the store.

"Want to help?" He smiled.

"Sure." She smiled back as he made room for her behind the table.

* * *

Bird looked around. "Lem is supposed to be film-
ing this, but he's over there laughing with Kenny
and Damon. I'll be back."

She walked over to Lem just as Ms. Wynn
walked up to the store.

"Happy Thanksgiving," everyone chorused.

"This is really great." Ms. Wynn looked around
at all the people. Tracy and Lemuel, I got some
news late last night and I wanted to come here
myself and tell you."

Lem's heart sank. "You sold our condo."

"Yes, I did sell it; escrow closed yesterday. And
normally this doesn't happen, but because your
sister inserted a special clause in the contract,
you'll get your entire deposit back." She smiled
broadly.

"You sold the condo?" Bird couldn't believe what
she was hearing. "And we're getting our money
back?"

"Yes."

Bird squealed and Lem looked at her like she was
crazy.

"You're glad we're not moving?"

"Yes." She locked a little sheepish as Lem pulled
her into his arms. "You said I always want stuff and
then change my mind. And you're right: I don't
want to move yet. Maybe one of these days, after
you become a millionaire and buy me a house next

door to Michael Jordan, but for now I'll just stay where I am." She smiled into his eyes. "If that's okay with you?"

Lem stuck out his chest and his beautiful smile lit up his face.

"My baby can have whatever she wants. Maybe we'll take a little of that ten thousand dollars and fix up the bathroom, if it's okay with the family. I'll get Kenny and Damon to help me."

"That sounds good to me, baby." Bird picked up Jay and went to tell her sisters the news.

Lem shook Ms. Wynn's hand enthusiastically. "Thank you so much."

"Ahmad. Come here." Teri grabbed him as he zipped by. "I have something for you." She handed him an envelope.

"What's this?"

"Read it. You're an intelligent young man."

He grinned as he ripped open the envelope, then read the memo inside.

"You're giving me your share in Mama Joe's house?" His eyes were wide with surprise.

"I sure am."

"Why?"

"It's time for some things to change around here. You're going to be moving into Mama Joe's house now, and I want you to have my share. I know how much you loved Mama Joe, and how much you love that house. I know you'll be responsible and see that the house is always taken care of."

"Wow."

"It's a lot of responsibility, but you've shown me that you are a wise young man. And I may not have any children to leave it to, and you've always been like a son to me."

"Thanks, Aunt Teri. I promise I won't let you down." He hugged her and ran to find his mother, with Teri following.

"Mom, Aunt Teri just gave me her share of Mama Joe's house—look!" He handed her the letter Teri had handwritten, deeding him her share of his grandmother's house.

Maxine quickly read it over. "Teri, what did you just do?"

"You read the letter. I want you guys to be able to move."

The rest of the family and Damon had also gathered.

"That's just wonderful." Maxine folded the letter back into the envelope and smacked Bird on the head with it. "Except your wishy-washy baby sister and her husband have decided they aren't moving."

"What?" Teri looked first at Bird and then at Lem. "Is this true?"

"Yes. They sold our condo. Isn't that wonderful?" Bird smiled at her sisters, who looked at her like she was crazy.

"Oh, come on. Y'all know how I am, and we got our ten thousand dollars back because of a special clause you inserted, Teri. Isn't that wonderful?"

"That's right, I did insert a thirty-day cure clause," Teri recalled slowly.

"Yeah, we know how you are, you're a spoiled brat—" Maxine began.

"And we wouldn't have you any other way, Miss Lake Shore Drive." Teri hugged both her sisters, while the others smiled. "You'll get there when you're supposed to."

"I hate to break this up, but everyone's ready to eat and they want us to bless the food," Kenny interjected.

"They don't want you to bless the food, Kenny, or we'll be out here all night long." Bird loved to tease him.

"Teri, take this back." Maxine handed Teri the letter she had given Ahmad.

"No, Maxine. I gave that to Ahmad and I meant it. I'm not going to take it back just because everyone decided not to move."

Maxine's mouth was still hanging open as the sisters and their families gathered around the microphone set up in the tent.

"Instead of the usual blessing, and in honor of the day, and especially since you have all come out to share your Thanksgiving with us . . ."

"Kenny, bless the food so the people can eat."

Bird was whispering, but she was standing near the microphone and everyone was able to hear her.

Soft laughter filled the room as Kenny finished blessing the food, then people began eating.

It was a beautiful sight. The banquet tables were covered with white linen tablecloths, and a simple floral centerpiece with a candle accented every table.

"As we were saying." Lem was in front of the mike now. "We just want everyone to share a few words of what they are most thankful for, and we'd like Teri, who's responsible for all of this, to begin."

People applauded as Teri took her place in front of the mike.

"I'm thankful that I'm alive. I'm thankful for my sisters and my family, and for the best friend in the world." She squeezed Damon's hand as everyone chorused "aah."

Bird was next. "I'm thankful for my husband and my baby boy, and knowing that no matter what, we'll always be together. And always, for my sisters and my family." She kissed Lem on the cheek and smiled.

Maxine followed. "I'm thankful for my husband, my dance partner for life, and my wonderful son, Ahmad; I'm so proud of the young man you've become. And for Kelly and Brooke, the most beautiful girls in the world. And last, but certainly not least, my wonderful sisters."

Kenny took the mike next. "I'm thankful for my wife, who loves me even when I'm a knucklehead. My children, my health, and all of you, my family."

Ahmad was standing next to his dad. "I'm thankful my Mom and Dad play kissy face."

Laughter filled the street, and it took everyone several minutes to quiet down.

"I'm also thankful that my Aunt Teri is still around to see me grow up and become a man she can be proud of, and I'm glad she's letting Damon hang out with the family. And—"

"Ahmad, don't you think you should let—"

"Kenny, let him finish," Maxine cut in. "Go ahead, baby." She had to smile, because he was telling everyone's business.

"I'm thankful for Dad, Uncle Lem, and Damon, who are showing me what it means to be a man. And I'm thankful that I'm still just a kid. And you know I love you, too, Aunt Bird."

"I know, baby." Her full lips curved into a smile.

"I'd just like to say I'm thankful for my beautiful wife." Lem took Bird by the hand and kissed her. "I'm still trying to understand why she chose me. I want to thank God for giving me the family I always wanted but never had. Teri and Maxine, y'all are my sisters; Kenny and Damon, y'all are my brothers."

The silence was thick with emotion when Damon finally spoke.

"I'm thankful to Teri for being the best friend I ever had."

It was a struggle for Bird not to make any type of response, but somehow she managed.

Damon continued, "I'm thankful to be here with you all today, and share this moment with a family I have come to know and love as my own." He raised his glass. "To family."

"To family," everyone chorused, and tapped their glasses together.

thirty-one

It was late afternoon by the time everyone was fed and the store was closed up. The family went to Teri's, where they gathered in front of the television to watch what was left of the football game.

Teri went into the kitchen for a bottle of champagne and Ahmad followed her.

"Aunt Teri, I need to give this back to you." He handed her the deed she had given him earlier.

"You don't have to give this back just because you aren't moving, Ahmad."

"I know Aunt Teri, but . . . I was thinking about what you said."

"What was that, sweetie?"

"You said I was like a son to you, and you may never have kids."

"That's right."

"Well, I haven't given up on you and Damon yet. So . . . if you still don't have any kids by the time I turn twenty-one, then I'll take it back." He left the envelope on the table and darted out of the kitchen before she could protest.

Teri shook her head and smiled, then picked up the champagne, slipped into the family room, and motioned for her sisters to follow her upstairs.

They curled up on Teri's bed with her in the middle. Bird lit the candles and turned on the music, while Maxine tiptoed back downstairs for three flutes. She popped the cork and poured the chilled bubbly into the glasses.

"This is better than passing the bottle around and each taking a swig." Maxine laughed as she gave each sister a flute.

"That would have been fine with me." Bird giggled.

"No, Miss Lake Shore Drive would at least need a straw." Teri laughed.

"Happy Thanksgiving!"

The sisters clicked glasses, and lay back to enjoy the champagne, the music, and one another.

"This Thanksgiving was the best ever," Bird sighed.

"It sure was," Maxine agreed. "We fed so many people."

"Just like Mama and Daddy used to do when we were little." Teri was smiling again. "This is the best Thanksgiving I ever had, too."

Bird admired the sparkling diamond tennis bracelet on Teri's wrist. She held her sister's arm in the candlelight and the diamonds sparkled like fire.

"And where did you get this?" she asked.

"Teri!" Maxine gasped. She pulled her sister's wrist closer for inspection.

"It's just a friendship bracelet."

"I don't see how you can call that bracelet *just* anything." Maxine was still in shock.

"So, we're extremely good friends. Okay?" Teri tried not to smile.

"So, what did you do to get it?" Bird teased.

"Bird . . . you are terrible." Teri giggled and tossed a pillow at her. Maxine fell out laughing beside her.

"I told you we didn't do anything. We're just . . ."

"Friends," the ladies chorused. They were all giddy with happiness, life, and love.

"Now, seriously." Teri lowered her voice. "There's one thing that I got for Thanksgiving that's even better."

"What?" Maxine and Bird asked, expecting to finally hear some juicy gossip.

"I got all my sisters with me."

As many as one in three
Americans with HIV...
DO NOT KNOW IT.

More than half of those
who will get HIV this year...
ARE UNDER 25.

HIV is preventable.
You can help fight AIDS.
Get informed. Get the facts.

www.knowhivaids.org
1-866-344-KNOW

GATHER UP
YOUR
LOVED ONES
FOR
THE LAUGHTER
AND TEARS
THAT IS

soul food
the series

The Complete First Season on DVD
A 5-Disc Set That Includes All 20 Episodes

Satisfy Your Appetite
June 24, 2003 on DVD

www.paramount.com/homeentertainment

NO LIMITS.

SFDVD1

Visit
❖ **Pocket Books** ❖
online at

---

www.SimonSays.com

Keep up on the latest new releases from your favorite authors, as well as author appearances, news, chats, special offers and more.

SIMON & SCHUSTER
A VIACOM COMPANY
www.SimonSays.com

Pocket
Books

2381-01